RECKONING

BLUE BLUE FINALE

THE BLUE BLOOD RETURNS SERIES
BOOK FIVE

STACY EATON

NITEWOLF NOVELS, LLC

CHAPTER ONE

KRISTIN

There was a dark cloud swirling above me that held a foreboding warning. It weighed heavily on my shoulders, and I wondered if this battle would be my last. I knew, for many, that it would be.

Over the last week, I thought about my life—a lot. From the moments I could remember as a child to my first husband, Trevor, who was human. My life would have taken a different direction if Trevor hadn't died in the line of duty so many years ago. Had I gotten pregnant with his child, the life I lived, *loved*, and knew so well would never have existed. I would have remained in the human world without being part of this one. It was a double-edged sword.

Would the life I had with Trevor have been enough? It could have been if I hadn't known this world existed. But I did know. Now, I looked at his death as a sign that there was a different road for me to follow. A route that led me to Julian, Alexander, and remembering a past that I hadn't been aware of when I was first Calista. A time long ago when I had fallen in love with the two men for the very first time.

It had been over a hundred years since Calista's life started—over eighty years since she first mated Julian. I glanced to the side of the bed, letting my gaze drift over Zander's sleeping face. His features were different, but inside, he was the same man I had loved so long ago. The two of us had been through so much. Different lives, other bodies, and many lovers, but destiny had brought us back to one another.

My heart filled with emotion, and I closed my eyes to stop the tears from springing forth. I refused to cry for what I might lose.

For so long, Julian and I had been forging our way through our lives, trying to find the love we had now. We had to wade through obstacles and decades to arrive here, and I was afraid our time would be cut short. I wanted centuries with the man, not just weeks.

Would my life always revolve around loving and losing? Trevor, Trent, and Alex were lost to me forever, but Zander was here. He was mine, and I refused to lose him—not now—not ever.

I climbed out of bed quietly and went to check on Briella. She lay on her back, her little hand fisted near her face, and her short bright-red hair standing in all directions.

What would life bring for her? Would I be alive to see it? Would I be here to watch her grow, fall in love, and experience the world? What kind of world would be there for her? Would she have to remain in hiding? Or would a time come when she could walk in public and experience everything I had growing up?

Would she even be able to go out in the sun? Would she manifest powers beyond what she could do now? All I knew was that she was in tune with Hugh and me. Thank God for Isaac being able to read her so well. How would I have learned that Briella was so special if it weren't for him? Other than waiting until the first time that she put her hand to my face to speak.

Despite where we were, she seemed to be able to feel through our formidable protection around the compound. Even as strong as I was, I could not reach out to Hugh from the inside. I had to be outside the compound to feel and communicate with him or Angelina.

Briella had felt Hugh's pain from within my body. What did that mean? What was this beautiful child of two reborns able to do? If Zander and I had a child, would that child exhibit extraordinary abilities too? I wanted to believe they would, and I wanted nothing more than to discover the possibilities and share a child with him, but now was not the time.

Once we survived this—if we survived this—I would ask Zander if he would have a child with me. I was pretty sure that he would, but I wanted to double-check.

Would we have the opportunity? Would we both survive? Would I be able to live if he didn't? I wasn't sure I could survive losing him—again. Could he survive losing me?

Briella shifted on her thin mattress and opened her crystal-clear ocean-blue eyes. They landed directly on mine, and I felt comfort engulf me. Was that her? Or was it just seeing my beautiful daughter gazing up at me? For three seconds, we locked eyes, and my heart calmed, and then she closed her eyes again and turned her head away before drifting back to sleep.

I stepped out of her room, closed the door quietly, and moved into our living area, where I went to the kitchen to make coffee. There was peace inside my soul, and I wanted to believe that it was Briella somehow telling me all would be well. Perhaps she could see the future, and she knew that I would survive—that we would survive.

A moment later, I felt him before I heard him, and then his hands slid around me as he nuzzled his face into my neck and kissed the sensitive skin there.

"Hello, my Mistress." His voice was husky from sleep, and I suppressed a shiver.

"Hello to you, my Master."

"Trouble sleeping?" He kissed under my ear.

"Some," I told him as I turned the coffee pot on, then turned in his arms and wrapped mine around his shoulders. "I'm sorry if I woke you."

"It's okay. I felt your unease when you got up, but you seem comforted now."

"I am. Briella helped me calm."

He raised a brow momentarily, then smiled and kissed my nose. "She's good at that, isn't she?"

I frowned slightly. "Do you really think she can do that? Or am I just making things up?"

He shook his head. "No, I think she can. She is amazing, Kris." He paused. "It makes me wonder what our child will be able to do."

"Our child?" I snickered. "Do you know something that I don't, Zander?"

He grinned. "Yeah, I know that as soon as this mess is over, I will knock you up."

"Knock me up, huh?"

He leaned forward and kissed me. "Yep. I don't want to admit it, but I am jealous that you share a child with Hugh and not me."

I laughed. "This is not a competition, Zander."

"I know, but after all this time, wouldn't it be great to share that? I mean, I have memories of us when Anastasia was born. I loved having a daughter with you."

"And to think that our daughter turned into my twin sister."

He rolled his eyes and growled playfully. "Don't remind me."

"How about when this is over, we discuss it again?"

He smiled. "Tell me something first. Do you want to have a child with me?"

I pulled him close to me. "Yes, Zander, I do. More than anything, I want us to share that connection."

"Then we will work on that when we get back."

"What if one of us doesn't return, Zander?"

"Kristin, sweetheart, we will survive this. I know you worry about that, but don't. We have a long life ahead of us and a world to rebuild for our people. We are going to do it. I know we are. I feel it in my very soul."

His voice was passionate, and I wished I could feel as positive as he did. I pulled away from him. "Well, I'm glad one of us feels so optimistic."

"We must feel that way, Kristin. You can't accept defeat before we even start the battle."

"But what if we fail, Zander? What if we are all killed? What if our way of life is over forever? We aren't just going up against a group of rogue vampires here. These are humans who are frail and have families. I took an oath so many years ago to protect them. I might not be a cop now, but I can't break that oath. If we storm in there and rile them up, the innocents will get caught in the crossfire. We are going up against a world of humans. Yes, we have a plan, but what if it becomes a trap? What if they imprison us all? If we are all there, how would we get free?"

"Whoa, Kristin, calm down. That's not going to happen." He took my face in his hands, speaking firmly. "I know your blood is still blue even after so many years. I understand your concern, but we will win and regain our lives with little to no collateral damage. We will be able to walk around outside again and live normal lives. We won't have to keep hiding forever."

"I hope that you are right, Zander. I really do, but I can't help but wonder who will survive this. I'm not stupid enough to think that all of us will. I can't imagine losing *anyone* after already losing so many."

"I know. It's difficult to stomach how many of our breed we have lost to the humans, but you can't think this way, Kristin. You must be strong and stay focused. If you give in to the worry, you will begin to second-guess yourself when you need to be at your strongest. There won't be time for that. All of this hinges upon *you* and your abilities."

"No! That's not true, Zander. This depends on all of us, including you. I can't be strong enough if something happens to you, and what if something happens to Angelina, Hugh, or Corbin? I won't be able to focus if I know one has fallen. I might not be strong enough to do what I must."

"You have to focus. No matter what happens, you keep going. You need to keep fighting through whatever they do to us, Kris. It's the only way our breed can survive. Even if something happens to me, turn to them and their strength. With so many of us reborns there, they won't know what hit them. With your ability to freeze the compound and compulsion, we will get in there with few casualties. Then we can deal with those who make the decisions once we are there. Those are the people we are most concerned with. Those are the people that give the commands and dictate how we are treated."

"Zander, I know everyone expects me to go in there and slay them all, but I don't want to do that. It will just prove their point that we are evil creatures."

"Evil? Jesus, Kris, they have been murdering thousands of our breed members. They are the fucking evil ones."

"Of course, they are monsters, and I don't want to be like them. I don't want to go in and kill them all."

"I'm not sure talking to them will be enough." He sighed. "I know you don't want to hurt anyone who hasn't directly hurt one of our people. I get that, but we have to show them we are serious, so if taking a few innocent lives is the cost, we must do it. We need to show them we are serious, and I don't think knocking on their front door and asking for a meeting over coffee and donuts will accomplish that."

I rubbed my hands over my face, crossed my arms over my chest, and leaned back against the counter. "I refuse to rush in there and slaughter people. I can't do it, Zander. I have to find a way to communicate with them and make them understand. We only want peace. We only want to live our lives."

Zander came to me and ran his hands up and down my arms. "If that's what you want to do, Kris, then you will find a way to do that. You never back down and always figure out the best way to handle things."

"Not always."

He lifted my chin to stare into my face. "No, not always, but when it counts, you do. I know you are scared, honey. I am too. All of us are scared, but we don't have a choice."

I sighed as he pulled me to his chest, and I put my ear to it and listened to the steady beat of his heart. "No, we don't have a choice."

"We will figure this out, Kristin. You aren't alone here."

"I know, but sometimes I feel like it all rests on my shoulders. Being the mistress is hard in the best of times, but now it is utterly overwhelming."

He kissed the top of my head. "I get it. I feel you agonizing over the decisions, but you aren't alone. You can let me shoulder some of this. I can help you make decisions and plans."

"I know you can, and maybe I need to do that."

He leaned back. "I think that's a good idea. Let me help you so that you don't feel so overwhelmed."

I smiled up at him, feeling just a tad bit better. Zander was intelligent and had many previous years of experience dealing with these types of problems when he was Julian. It shouldn't have taken me this long to figure out that he could help me. He was initially born and bred to be the master, after all.

"Okay, I'll let you help, and I know precisely what you can start doing."

"What's that?" he asked as he shifted back to put distance between our bodies.

I reached for the tie on my robe and undid it. "You can make love to your mate."

A feral growl ripped from his throat as he speared one hand through my hair to cup my head and curled the other arm around my waist to pull me to his body. "That is one task I will always be willing to do."

CHAPTER TWO

CORBIN

Maybe I was selfish to suggest such a thing as triple bonding. When I first thought about it, I wondered if Hugh would go for it. I was careful to word it that I was concerned that a mating between them might diminish Angelina's power. Not that I knew that. I had no fucking clue, but I knew that Hugh was young enough that he would probably be concerned about that—not knowing any different.

I was right. That had been something on Hugh's mind already, and he told me that was one reason he hadn't taken her the first chance he could. Besides being the nice guy, he wanted Angelina to make the final decision.

Well, she had. That decision skyrocketed my lust for her. I took a chance that Hugh would be on board with all of it. At first, I wasn't sure he would, but he didn't push me away when I came to him and kissed him, and he sure as hell didn't shove me off when I grabbed his cock and stroked it.

I had felt an explosive blast of desire from Angelina, which maybe sparked Hugh to accept and continue. Perhaps he desired her so much that knowing she was into this kept him going for fear of rejection.

Taking Angelina from behind while she rode Hugh was even

better than being with her while she took Gideon. What made it different and so much more fucking incredible was the three of us sharing blood. The power I felt spread faster through my veins the more I drank until I thought I would burn from the insides.

The orgasm that took us over was like a fucking volcano when it erupted. All three of us were caught in the rippling waves of lava as it barreled over. It was the most intense thing I had ever experienced, and after my long life, that was saying a lot.

When Angelina began to laugh, Hugh and I looked at each other.

"Did we break her? Do something wrong?" he asked silently.

"No, I think we did just about everything right."

When she opened her eyes and the bright white radiated out, I felt the tidal wave of power wash through her and knew this was a damn good decision.

What Lena said next was an even better decision. "I want that again, but first, I want to watch you two." She leaned back against the headboard and smiled one of her sexy-as-fuck grins.

Hugh was tense at first, but the more I worked on him, the more he got into it. In fact, it didn't take him long to get more into it than I could have imagined. His large hand took hold of my sack and tugged, and I almost lost it. I shoved him back and bent over his waist before I sucked him deep into my mouth. A growl vibrated through Hugh, and I felt Lena's desire pulsing off her, making it even more enjoyable. I deep-throated him a few times and was about to do it again when he shoved me away hard enough that I almost toppled off the bed.

He chuckled as I shifted to my side, and then he practically dove over me and lifted my cock. "You want to play dirty? I can do that too." Before I knew what was happening, he sucked my cock into his mouth. My head fell back on my shoulders as he swirled his tongue over the tip as if he were a pro with years of experience. Maybe he was; I had no clue.

A few moments later, Angelina was crawling in between us. "As incredible as it is to watch, I feel left out."

"We can't have that," I replied as I shifted her around and had her sit on my face.

The second round was even better than the first. Afterward, we collapsed onto the bed, exhausted and sated for the moment.

"How do you feel?" Hugh asked Lena.

"Very satisfied," she purred.

Hugh chuckled as I asked, "Glad to hear that, but what about what's going on inside?"

"Better than I have ever felt before," she said with a satisfied smile. "Every inch of my body is tingling. It's like the blood is rebuilding my insides."

"Good," Hugh replied and yawned.

"What about you?" she asked Hugh.

He stared at the ceiling momentarily. "Pretty fucking wired at the moment, although I also feel tired, and would it be weird to say I am hungry?"

I chuckled. "No, man, I'm starving. Why don't I order food to be brought up to the room?"

After the other two approved, I cleaned up, pulled on my pants, and went into the other room. I had suggested doing this for more than just ordering food. I needed a moment to digest this new situation. I figured Angelina and Hugh would also need time to discuss the matter in private.

I ordered an assortment of items, unsure what everyone would want, and then I poured myself a drink and threw it back. Man, being mated to one person was intense, but now coupled with two—holy shit!

I had to admit that when I had mated to Angelina, I had felt my power swell, but now, it was like I had electricity running through my veins instead of blood—like I was plugged into an electrical outlet without wires.

I wandered back to the door; Angelina was lying in bed alone. I glanced toward the bathroom to find the door closed.

"Everything okay?"

"Yeah, Hugh said he wanted a shower."

"Is he alright with what happened?"

She shrugged a little bit. "Maybe a little off-kilter. That was all new to him. I don't think he expected to like it as much as he did." She paused. "I know that being with another man is not new to you, but do you enjoy that sort of thing?"

"Yep, I've been around for over a hundred years and tried it all. Some things a few times." I waggled my brows her way.

"I hear that." She sat up higher in the bed. "How do you feel?"

I grinned like a fool and chuckled. "Like I'm connected to a high-powered generator."

"Yeah, me too."

The door to the bathroom opened, and Hugh stepped out. His gaze locked on mine, and he tried to look away, but it took him a second. I didn't miss how his gaze drifted to my waist and my unbuttoned pants before he finally tore his eyes away. Was he regretting what we had done or wishing for more?

"Food should be here soon." I picked my shirt up off the floor and asked, "How are you feeling, Hugh?"

"Honestly?" He peered my way momentarily. "I feel like I'm high. Like I'm on a wave, drifting at a wild rate of speed. I'm waiting for the crash."

"Well, I guess we can all say that the extra power is there for all of us."

"Does this mean that my abilities will be stronger?" Hugh asked.

I shrugged. "I don't know. Try it out."

He laughed. "It's kind of hard to when you are both right here. You forget that I can see through the eyes of people I have shared blood with."

I thought about that for a second. "Okay, what about Kristin? You've been mated to her, so her blood bond should still be strong even though that mating is broken. Can you feel her? Can you see through her eyes?"

He closed his eyes and then shook his head after a few seconds. "It's hard to get outside of the shield around this place."

I started toward him, and he tensed. "Relax, I'm not going to bend you over the bed and have my way with you." I gave him a wicked grin to tell him I would very much like to do that. I chuckled and put my hand on his shoulder. "I just want to give you a boost of power. Try it now."

I focused my power on Hugh; a light-green glow came from where I touched him.

He concentrated for a few seconds, and then his eyes popped open. "Jesus! I can feel her, but just barely," he said, his voice growing husky as if he were struggling, and he clenched his eyes to focus again.

Angelina crawled to the end of the bed and put her hand on his back; the light green grew brighter, and Lena and I grinned like two kids on Christmas morning after Santa dropped off a shitload of toys.

"Holy fuck! I can see. What the hell is she doing?" he asked himself as he continued watching something we could not see. "Oh my god! She just froze the entire compound."

"What?" Lena jerked her hand away from Hugh in alarm. "Why would she do that?"

Hugh turned to Lena, breaking the connection as my hand fell away. "She wasn't doing anything to hurt them. I think Kris and Zander were testing her ability. She was able to stop everyone inside the compound. That's pretty damn impressive."

"But how do you know that's what she was doing?"

"Because I saw what she saw. She was holding Zander's hands, and they were glowing like that time we had touched her at the club, only so much brighter, and then she looked at the virtual monitors that showed the complex, and everyone was frozen in place. It was like someone put the television on pause."

"Wow," I stated. "That is impressive. About how many people are there?" "Just over eight hundred, I think," he responded.

"That has to take a lot of power." I studied Angelina. "Do you think you could do that?"

"Freeze almost a thousand people? No. I doubt that."

"I bet you could. Your power is strong now, Lena, and with Hugh and me to help you, I bet you could do what your sister does."

"Maybe, but we don't know that." She got off the bed and headed toward the bathroom. "I'm going to take a shower before the food arrives."

After we heard the water turn on, I glanced at Hugh. "We okay?"

Hugh turned to me, opened his mouth, and then closed it before he frowned. "I'm not exactly sure how I feel."

"Well, let me ask you this, and be honest. Did you enjoy it?"

He was quiet for a moment, and a muscle ticked in his jaw before he answered softly, "Yeah, I guess I did. More than I probably should or ever thought I would."

I shrugged. "Then let it go at that. Don't put more on it than there is. We did what we did because Lena liked it and wanted us to. Our breed is very sexual. You know that. It's not unheard of for us to have sex with both sexes. It's no big deal."

He laughed as he stood up. "No big deal? You know that's the first time another guy has sucked my dick, and—and I reciprocated."

"But you liked it. What's the big deal?"

He stepped forward, getting in my face. "The big deal is I *did* like it, and I can't fucking stop thinking about it."

"Because you want it again?"

"Yeah, because I do. God, help me, but I fucking do."

I curled my hand around the back of his neck. "Relax, Hugh. It will happen again, as often as you want it to, but right now, we all need to eat and see what else we can do. After that, I don't know what ability I might have, but the fact that you could see through the mistress's eyes while she is underground in a protective compound is pretty fucking amazing."

He stepped back, frowning slightly. "Yeah, I guess it is."

"You guess? Dude, that's incredible. You'll be able to check on her to make sure she is alright. Even if a barrier separates us."

"Right, that is good." He thought for a moment. "What can you do?"

"That's a good question, Hugh. Honestly, I have no clue. I never figured it out after I mated to Angelina, so I guess we shall see what presents itself now."

"Do you feel differently?"

"Of course. I feel like a low voltage is running through my veins, heating my blood."

Hugh thought about that for a second as he rubbed a hand over his jaw. "Maybe it has something to do with electricity? I mean, I feel the power deep in my body now. I felt the electrical buzz when we first connected, but not now. Maybe I felt that because of you."

I considered that for a few seconds. "Perhaps."

Hugh turned and looked at the light on the side table. "See if you can turn it on."

"Turn on a light? Of course, I can turn on a light."

"No, with your mind. See if you can do it by thinking about it."

I chuckled. "Why?"

"Because maybe you can control electricity. Just try it, Corby."

I rolled my eyes. "Jesus, not you, too, with that fucking nickname." Hugh snickered, and I turned away from him. I had nothing to lose by trying it. I went to stand near the lamp and stared at it for a moment, pulling power up from inside of me and focusing on the light. Nothing happened, and I frowned. "Nothing. Got any other ideas?"

Hugh came up behind me. "Try touching the light."

I focused on the light again and pulled my power harder. I felt crackling under my skin and began to reach for the lamp. At the same time, Hugh put his hand on my back, and with my fingers only four inches from the light, a bolt of electricity came from deep inside of me and struck the light.

The light turned on, grew brighter, and then exploded. At the same time, Hugh yelped and flew back against the wall behind me with a thunderous crash.

All the lights in the room went off, and I heard Angelina yell, "What the fuck was that?"

I rushed to Hugh, who was trying to sit up with a dazed look in his eyes.

The bathroom door whipped open, and Angelina rushed out, a towel wrapped around her wet body, her hair full of bubbles from the shampoo. "Why are all the lights out?" She stared at Hugh. "And why is he on the floor? Did you hit him?"

"No, I didn't hit him!" I snapped her way.

Hugh laughed as he started to get off the floor. I offered him my hand, and he stared at it momentarily and then shook his head. "No, man, thanks. One shock is enough."

"You shocked Hugh?" Angelina asked, confused.

"Not on purpose," I replied, staring at my hands.

I could hear someone in the hallway asking why the power was off, and Hugh and I looked at each other and started laughing. "Maybe that was a little too much power," he said.

"I was trying to test something. I told Hugh it felt like I had electricity in my veins, and he told me to turn on the light."

Hugh laughed and went to inspect the lamp on the nightstand. "At first, it didn't work, so I thought maybe if I touched him and gave him some of my power, it might help him as he did me. I guess it worked a little too well."

"It gave me too much, and we weren't expecting it." I chuckled. "I zapped the light and Hugh at the same time. I might have blown out all the power in the building."

Angelina cocked her head. "Well, look at that. I think that might be handy when we attack the White House."

Hugh and I exchanged a look. "It just might. You'll have to tell Kristin about that."

"I'm going to finish my shower now, in the dark, mind you. Why don't you two have a seat and stop playing with things before you bring the building down?" She gave us a look like she was scolding two errant children, and after she returned to the bathroom, Hugh and I started to laugh again.

This triple mating might have just been the best idea of my life.

CHAPTER THREE

ZANDER

It had been over three weeks, and all the plans were underway. Kristin and I worked side by side. It allowed her to shift some of the stress from her shoulders and put it on mine. We also discovered we worked very well together—not that I doubted we would. I looked forward to ruling beside her for several hundred years once this was over.

We had ended up giving the human-turned another week, as some were still struggling. Unbeknownst to us, Portage had added more human-turned to the mix. Kristin almost lost her shit until I reminded her it was for a good reason. In total, we now had one hundred and ninety-six human-turned. One hundred and three were women with different abilities.

Angelina, Hugh, and Corbin had stayed on top of what was happening and had given us regular updates. They seemed excited about what was happening over there, which made Kris and me feel better about the decision.

Hugh also told Kristin that he had a surprise for her, and even though she tried to get it out of him, he said that she needed to see it to believe it. Kristin got annoyed and did a lot of eye-rolling, but eventually, she stopped dwelling and muttering about it.

Kris had finally told the compound that she could unlock the doors early and that what they were about to attempt would be dangerous and deadly. Only the strongest occupants would go, leaving enough people behind to protect those who remained at the compound.

Right now, people were saying goodbye to their loved ones and friends because we would be moving out soon.

Thirty of us would depart the compound and head to the hotel location. Thirty more would head south to Atlanta, fifty to New York, and another two hundred were heading west to different areas. They would have three days to get to their locations, make final plans, then get into place. The strikes would take place simultaneously across the nation.

Gideon had gathered over three thousand of the breed from around the country to fight this war, and we hoped we would come out on top, and once this fight was over, we could move on with life again.

It was my understanding that Portage had another two thousand of his followers that were willing to fight. For this, we were all putting aside our grievances and working as one. The battle wasn't about who would rule but whether we would survive. I hoped that we would not only survive but thrive once this was over and done with.

I stood at the door of our bedroom and watched Kristin with Briella. Over the last few weeks, my relationship with Kristin had flourished beyond belief—despite the grave circumstances. We worked as a team, loved as a passionate couple, and enjoyed every moment we could with her daughter.

As much as I wished to be the child's father, I wasn't, and I hoped that once this battle was finished, Kristin and I didn't waste time having one of our own. I kept a close eye on her to make sure that she hadn't already conceived. If she had, there would be no way that I would want her to attempt what we planned.

There was a knock at the door, and then it opened immediately after. Isaac stepped in and nodded at me. "Master, they say it is time."

Kristin sighed and then nuzzled Briella's head as she stood and approached us. "Time for momma to go, sweet pea. You be good for Isaac."

Briella squealed slightly as her gaze locked on her mother's face, and then she put both of her hands on her mother's cheeks. Kristin closed her eyes, inhaling deeply as something passed between them.

Kristin frowned as she stared at her daughter, and then she smiled slightly. "Your message has been received." Briella continued to stare at her mother, and then Kris chuckled. "I promise your father will come back once this is over." She smiled again at her daughter before kissing her brow and coming to my side.

I ran my knuckles over Briella's cheek. "Stay sweet, little girl." I kissed her brow, and then Isaac was there to take her.

"I wish that I could go," Isaac said huskily. "I feel as if I should be there fighting beside you."

Kristin laid her hand on his arm. "Isaac, your job is much more important than just fighting. You are right where you need to be. I need you to keep her safe so I don't worry about her the whole time. You vowed to watch her always."

"Yes, Mistress. You have my word."

Kristin held her daughter's hand for a moment longer, a wistful look in her eyes. I tried to read what was happening inside her brain, but she was locked down. After a few seconds, she quickly turned and walked away. I didn't miss the moisture in her eyes as she made a beeline for the door.

"Thank you, Isaac," I told him as I followed Kristin.

Isaac reached out and grabbed my arm as I went to pass. "Protect her, Master. Briella is worried about what she will face. She has seen the danger and knows her mother will be hurt." He looked concerned.

"Hurt?" I glanced at the door to see Kristin was gone. "How badly, Isaac?"

"Badly. Briella believes her mother will survive, but it will take all who are reborn to make that happen. Be ready."

I stared at him for a long moment, then touched Briella. "Thank you for the warning. I will protect her with my life."

I stepped out of the room to find Kristin long gone. For a moment,

I stood there, staring at the closed door to the suite and wondering if I should tell Kristin what I had learned, but I decided that I needed to keep this to myself until the time came. I pushed the thoughts of Kristin getting injured into the recesses of my mind and locked them down tightly as I made my way down the hall.

The garage was hopping when I arrived there. Transport vehicles were pulled out of storage, and supplies were added. The night before, twenty human-turned had arrived at our location. They were all air shields, and they would protect the transports as they left here and traveled. There would be two for every vehicle so they could take turns while traveling. To any human, the transports would not exist.

Everyone gathered around as Kristin came out to stand on the loading dock. The area grew quiet as Kristin looked over them all, and I stood beside her, my hand on her lower back, trying not to think about what I had just heard.

"What you are all about to embark on will decide our future. It will determine if our breed will exist in the open or if we will spend the rest of our lives hiding in the shadows of the night, always fearing what the humans will do to us if we are found." She paused and let her gaze slide over the group thoughtfully. "Some of you will not return, and I want to thank you all now. Not only for what you are about to do but for what you have done for me during these tumultuous years. I respect and appreciate every single one of you for the sacrifices you have given Alex, me, and our people. I want you to know that the decision to war with the humans was a difficult one to make."

She hesitated and took a deep breath before continuing. "If you fall in this battle, please know that your sacrifice will not be in vain. You will be remembered always in my heart and in our history." She paused again. "I know we don't want to dwell on those things, but we must be prepared in case they occur."

Many people nodded and looked around at others with them as she continued. I wondered how many of them were thinking about who might not return—I knew I was. She smiled as if she were announcing good news. "Now, let us take back our lives and our world and give them the reckoning that they never saw coming!"

A roar of approval rushed across the room with cheers and fist pumps, and then everyone moved to their designated transports after saying goodbye to loved ones who would stay behind.

Garrett stepped forward, wrapping his arms around his mother. He spoke softly to her, but I was close enough to hear. "I love you, Mom. I know I don't tell you that very often, but I do."

She touched his face. "And I love you, Garrett. Help Ben and the other elders with our people. If we do not return, do as they say until you are of age to take over officially. I have entrusted our people to you."

"I will do my best." He nodded, then shook my hand. "Zander, I look forward to you returning and bringing Corbin so I can get to know my brothers better."

"I look forward to it too."

I took Kristin's hand, and we headed toward the transport bus we would be on, followed closely by Joshua.

Rane opened the compound doors, and one by one, we left. For now, the mood was excited and jovial. I knew that that mood would turn deadly and serious in a few days.

Two hours later, our group arrived at the hotel where Portage was holed up with Angelina and the rest of the crew. The hotel was above capacity now, and people would be sharing rooms. Cots had been set up in some of the smaller dining areas so everyone would have a place to rest and prepare.

When we stepped off the transport bus, Angelina was waiting with Hugh and Corbin. Had she not decided whom she would mate with? I knew Kristin had asked her, but she said she would explain her decision in person.

Kristin and her sister hugged tightly, and then Kristin reared back and stared at her in surprise. "Why do you smell of two men?"

Angelina glanced around, looking rather proud of herself. "Because I am mated to two men."

Kristin looked as surprised as I was. "How is that possible?" I asked what I knew Kristin was wondering.

"Let's just say it is a little kinky." Angelina smirked, and Hugh and Corbin laughed beside her.

"Are you serious?" Kristin asked. "You are literally mated to both of them?"

"Yep, and not just me, but they are mated to one another too. Wait till you see what they can do. You know that Hugh could see through my eyes when I was out of the compound, right?"

"Yes."

"Yeah, well, he could see you *inside* the compound. He's been telling us all kinds of things that you have been doing." She grinned cheekily and glanced my way. "I guess I'm not the only one into kinky these days."

I laughed and turned to Hugh. "You can really do that?"

"Yeah, with the help of these two, I could see what you were doing. I couldn't hear anything, and sometimes it was only small pieces of time. It still only seems to work on people I have fed from, but it's a pretty cool tool."

"Interesting," Kristin said as if she wasn't so sure about all of this. She shifted to Corbin. "What can you do?"

Angelina laughed. "Oh, please do not ask him to show you right now. I think Portage would blow a gasket if the power went out again at the hotel."

Corbin grinned. "I will show you later, but I think it will be very useful. I can channel electricity. The first time I tried, I about put Hugh through a wall while taking out all the circuits at the hotel."

Kristin's brows rose. "That sounds intriguing, Corbin. You will have to tell us more later." She shifted to Angelina. "And you, what has this crazy triple mating done to you?"

"Given me some incredible sex," she stated, and Hugh actually blushed as his gaze cut to Corbin's. Did I even want to know? I didn't think so.

Kristin rolled her eyes. "I'm serious, Angelina. What has changed in you?"

"Well, let's go inside, and I will show you."

"I'd rather you tell me," Kristin said under her breath but followed her sister.

When we reached the lobby, Angelina turned to her sister. "Okay, freeze them all."

Kristin glanced around. "What?"

"I want you to freeze them. You know, compel them to stop moving."

"I know what you want. Why?"

Angelina looked annoyed. "Because I want to show you something."

Kristin, who looked slightly more annoyed, pulled her power forward, her eyes and hands glowing slightly as she spoke. "Freeze." Since we had been practicing that at the compound, she found it easier to do it alone.

All the occupants of the lobby stopped moving, and Angelina turned away from her sister, closed her eyes, and focused for a second before she said, "Release."

Everyone returned to moving, although quite a few looked at us as if they weren't too happy to have been compelled to stop. I had a feeling it wasn't the first time she had done something like that to them.

"I already knew you could break compulsion, Angelina."

"Yes, but I can break *any* compulsion someone puts out, and I can't be compelled."

Kristin turned to her sister, her eyes glowing that eerie silver. "Stand on one foot."

Angelina started to pick up her foot and then stomped it back to the ground. "Don't do that shit! I just told you that you couldn't compel me."

"But you started to do it."

"Yeah, because you said to, but not because you were attempting to compel me."

Kristin shifted her gaze to Corbin and Hugh. "Stand on one foot."

They looked at one another, smiled, and then turned back to Kris.

"It doesn't work on us either," Corbin said with a laugh. "But your eyes are freaking incredible. They look like liquid silver."

She ignored his statement. "That's good that you both share her ability. Can you handle electricity, Lena?"

Angelina winced. "I'm not very good with that. I started an itsy-bitsy fire. I'd rather not try it again."

Hugh rubbed a hand over his mouth to hide the laugh.

"That was no itsy-bitsy fire, Lena." Corbin grinned. "Luckily, we were in the kitchen, and the sprinklers came on. The chef was furious since they were making the main meal."

Just then, Portage approached us looking rather indignant. "Your sister and her boy toys are making a menace of this place. I sure hope that you can keep them in line since they can't seem to do it themselves."

Behind his back, Angelina made faces, and I tried not to bark out the laugh that was building in my chest.

"They are adults. They know how to behave." Kristin gave them a stern look, making me want to laugh harder.

Instead, I changed the topic. "How are things going on your end, Joseph?"

"Fine, everything that I needed to do is completed now, son."

I glared at him when he used that term, and he quickly apologized as Kristin continued the conversation.

"I'd like to see the human-turned," she stated.

"I was waiting for you to arrive to head over myself. I am sure you will be happy with their progress."

"Just watch out for the fire starters. They almost caught Angelina's blouse on fire," Hugh advised us.

"Little bitch almost saw her last day on earth—again," she said playfully.

"Save the death threats for the humans," I told her as we followed Portage to a door leading to the basement. He led us to a tunnel under the building to a warehouse behind the hotel.

When we arrived, all the human-turned were seated in the center of the warehouse, and Gabe and Olivia stood before them talking.

Olivia waved us over. "For those who have never met them, this is Mistress Kristin Armstrong and Master Zander Armstrong."

We took in the group, and I watched Kristin smile. "Thank you," Kristin said as she stepped forward. "I appreciate your sacrifices and how hard you have been working. Your abilities will help us win back our freedom and give us a better future, including you."

Olivia and Gabe broke them into groups, and we went from one to the other, watching the kinds of things they could do. From lifting earth and building walls that could hold people back to pulling water out of the air to fill containers, blowing things up with the air, and shielding other things like the building and the transports we had been in earlier. They were all equally impressive, but the most impressive ones could manifest fire with just a thought.

Watching a vampire pull a fireball out of thin air both amazed and terrified me. I sure hoped we didn't need to use them, but it was nice knowing they were on our side if we did.

We discussed plans for the next two days and relaxed the best we could. As we all retired to our rooms to sleep on the final day, I pulled Kristin into my arms. I had worked hard not to dwell on what Isaac had said to me, but those thoughts surfaced occasionally as I watched her work. She was always too busy to notice, and I was glad. I didn't want to have to explain them to her. "We're going to do it, Kris."

"I know—at least, I think we will. There is a lot that can go wrong."

"True, but there is a lot that can go right."

I held her for a long moment, and then she lifted her face to mine. "Make love to me like it's our last chance ever."

I stared into her worried eyes, then caressed her face. Once again, those thoughts tried to rear their ugly head, but I held them back. "No, but I'll make love to you like it's the first day of the rest of our lives—because it is."

With that, I lifted her into my arms and carried her to the bed, making sure to love her with everything I had. As much as I wanted my statement to be accurate, I knew hers might also be dead-on—especially after the warning I'd received from Briella through Isaac.

CHAPTER FOUR

GIDEON

Being at the compound with the mistress and master had been a heady experience. I had been accepted into the fold quickly and without question. The second day I was there, I attended all the meetings with them and the elders.

I had been a leader previously in our underground home under the building, but now I had a different role. I was being led by the hand of the mistress and thriving on it. I watched everything Kristin or Zander did, committing decisions to memory and explaining why those decisions were the ones to win. I knew I would never be at their level, but I was a good leader and hoped to one day have a greater responsibility to our people.

The start of the day was for meals and meeting people, then exploring the incredible complex built into a mountain. At the end of the day, I relaxed and got to know the people, especially the sentinels, but none as well as Paxton.

Paxton and I had spent every moment we could together since I arrived. Within days, I felt like I had met my future—with Paxton and the breed.

I appreciated that Kristin was willing to listen to my suggestions and encouraged me to bring my knowledge of living out in the world these last several months to the table. She even put me in charge of communicating directly with all the other group leaders nationwide. It was a position I never expected to have—especially so soon—and I swore to her and Zander that I would do everything I could for them and the breed.

Paxton and I were lying in bed together the night before we left when she said, "I think we should mate."

"Um." I laughed nervously. "What made you say that now?"

She rolled to her stomach and looked at me. "Because we don't know what the future may hold, Gid. We should take what we have and run with it."

I was surprised to hear her say that. I mean, I knew she liked me, but not enough to want to mate with me. "We should discuss this after we finish our task."

She stared at me for a long moment, her auburn hair in messy disarray from our latest escapade. "Have you ever been mated before?"

"I have."

"What happened to her?"

"She broke our mating when she mated my best friend."

Her eyes widened. "Oh, shit! That sucks! How long ago was that?"

"About thirty years ago." I paused. "What about you?"

She shook her head. "I never found anyone I liked enough or wanted to have that close to me in my life."

I chuckled. "And you like me enough to suggest such a thing?"

She shrugged a sexy shoulder. "Maybe."

"Well, I'm honored, Pax, but I think we should keep our heads in the game here. You and I are going to be on opposite sides of the country. I don't want to be worried about you while I'm trying to focus on what I need to do."

"You wouldn't have to be worried about me. I can take care of myself, Gideon. I have been doing that for over sixty years."

I cupped her cheek. "I know you can. That's what I like about you. How about we table this discussion until after we win? Then when we get back, we can discuss it again."

"Are you open to the idea?"

It took me a moment to reply. "Are you interested in mating someone because you are worried about what will happen?"

She shook her head. "No, that is not why I suggested it. This isn't just a knee-jerk reaction to the upcoming battle. It just feels right. Are you not interested? You can tell me, and I won't be hurt. It is pretty soon."

Was I interested? Yes, which surprised the hell out of me. "Oddly enough, I am."

"Oddly enough?" She chuckled.

I leaned on my elbow, so my face was closer to hers. "Yeah, I am. I like you a lot, Paxton, and I think we could have something great."

"I do too," she whispered toward me as her eyes sparkled in my direction.

"Then we will talk about it again when this is over."

"Okay, so no more talking tonight." She gave me a sassy smile. "But I would like to have sex one more time."

"Only one more time?" I asked as I pulled her face closer.

"At least." She breathed toward me before I took her lips. As I made love to her again, I momentarily thought about Angelina and all she had given me. I will forever be grateful to her for giving me back this part of my life. I had assumed I would forever be alone, but now, I had Paxton and possibly a future with her.

That is if we both made it back.

PAXTON WOULD BE GOING EAST, and I would be heading west. My group of fifty had the farthest to travel since we had to go to California. As we waited for Kristin to give us last words, Paxton stood beside me, her arm touching mine.

As with many of those around us, there was anxiety under her thick-skinned surface. As the group broke apart to head to our vehicles, she turned to me. "We have a date to talk, don't forget that."

I stared at her, falling into her soft-brown eyes. I grabbed her face and brought our mouths together for a long passionate kiss goodbye. I stared at her when we finished. "I won't forget. It's a date, Paxton. Stay safe."

Without another word, she spun and walked away, and I loaded into the bus with the others in my group. I smiled to myself as I got settled. If things worked out, I had an exciting future to plan.

For now, I had to focus on what needed to happen. On our trip, we had two human-turned shields protecting us at night, and it was just another bus to anyone on the road. No one could feel us or would think twice about us as we drove past. We also had two compelled human bus drivers who would trade off so that we could keep going during the day. Our only stops were two hours long to recharge the batteries on the transport, and during that time, we were all anxious as we sat quietly and waited.

It took over two days to arrive at our location, and I contacted Clayton as soon as we did to let him know all was well on this side of the country. He informed me that, by some miracle, all the transports had reached their destinations safely.

It was time to get hooked up with the leaders here and others in the nearby states overseeing key locations during our reckoning, as the mistress was calling it.

Things were going smoothly here, as with the other groups I had been in contact with. Never in the history of our breed had something like this been done. What we were about to attempt would go down not only in our history books but those books for humans also. Who would be the victors? Did the humans have other weapons they could use against us that we weren't aware of?

The night before we were to strike, I spoke to Paxton on the phone. Even though we had a bond, it wasn't strong enough to communicate this far apart. Our conversation was short, but before we hung up, she paused. "Don't forget we have a date."

"I won't, Pax. Be careful, and I look forward to that date."

"I do, too, Gid." She paused again, and I wondered if she was thinking the same thing I was. Should I tell her how I felt about her? Or would it be best to wait? I wasn't sure I was in love with her, but I knew I cared about her. Was she thinking the same thing?

"Hey, save whatever you have on your mind for when we see each other again," I said huskily.

"If that is what you want." Her voice was low, almost disappointed.

I laughed. "No, I want to have you under me again, but I don't think we should express our feelings right now."

"You're right." She sighed and lifted a brow in question, "So, how about I just tell you to keep your ass safe so I can have you back in my bed?"

I laughed again. "I think that is good to say, and that goes for you too."

"You got it. Talk to you soon, Gideon."

"Talk to you soon, Paxton."

After I hung up, I wondered if maybe I should have told her how I felt. I had a feeling that she knew, which would have to do. I still had a dozen more calls to make so I could get a couple of hours of sleep before we got moving.

Somehow, I managed to sleep, or at least close my eyes and rest a bit. When it was time to go, we loaded into the box truck. The truck would take us toward the state capitol building we were designated to hit. Our group had the most complicated job, striking in full daylight. Those on the east coast were lucky since it was winter and the sun was setting. We had to do it in full daylight for all of us to attack simultaneously.

We were lucky it was overcast today, and storms were forecasted, but I knew some of our teams were not so lucky.

Kristin had been wise to shift people around the country. The older members were closer to the east coast, while the younger members were on the west. In my group, most breed members were young enough to withstand sunshine for a short period without too much pain. We even had members of our breed that had not yet transitioned.

To be safe, we all wore protective clothing. It was a little restrictive, but with the way our adrenaline, and bloodthirst, would be coursing through our veins, we shouldn't have trouble doing what we needed to do—and that was to fight for our lives.

We were in place, and I glanced at my watch. We had five minutes until it was time to go, and I tried to calm my nerves. It wasn't that I was anxious we would lose. If we did, then we did. It was because there was so much at stake, and I prayed that if we didn't take control of our objective, others would be able to do so and give us enough leverage to take back our lives.

With my earpiece for the communication device in place, I listened to the rest of our group check-in. Everyone was in place now, and the once-gay chatter amongst us was silent.

Right before the door to the truck opened, I closed my eyes and prayed to whatever God overlooked us. Please let us survive this and regain our right to live normal lives. Do not let us have suffered so much to have it all taken from us forever.

I opened my eyes and squinted into the bright light as the liftgate began to go up. It was time to begin.

CHAPTER FIVE

HUGH

I was awake before Angelina and Corbin, and before I left the suite, I stopped and studied Corbin sleeping on the couch. With all the people at the hotel, the three of us were sharing one suite now. The first night, we had slept in the same bed, Angelina between us. Since then, Corbin had chosen to sleep on the sofa. I wasn't sure of that meaning, but I was somewhat confused about many things now. When I let myself dwell over it, it blew my mind that I was not only finally mated to Angelina but also to Corbin.

Corbin stirred, and I slipped out of the suite before I got caught watching him. I'd never been attracted to another man before. I hadn't ever wondered what it would be like to kiss another man, much less touch a man intimately. Yet I watched him, wanting him in a way I had never thought possible. Was that only because of my bond with him and Angelina?

Or had Corbin somehow unlocked another side of my nature? I had to assume that was because of our mating bond, not me secretly craving the touch of a man.

If someone had asked me a year ago to have sex with a man, I would have either laughed in their face or beat them silly. However, being with Corbin seemed different—especially with Angelina with us. Would I want to have sex with Corbin alone? I wasn't sure, but the flutter in my groin at that thought made me wonder.

As I recalled being with the two of them, I realized it was comforting in a way, and as much as I didn't want to admit it—exciting as hell. Everything was as it should be when we were together—not just in bed but in the same room.

When Corbin touched me and Angelina watched, it blew my mind and turned up the desire to a level I wasn't familiar with. The feel of his rough, strong hands on my body made me almost weak in the knees and had me wishing for things I wasn't sure I wanted—although maybe I secretly craved. Was my depravity even more profound than I had once thought?

Even though I had touched Corbin and tasted him, I still hadn't dared to touch him as he did me—freely and without pause. Would I one day want to sink my cock deep into him, as I did to Angelina?

The thought sent a shiver of desire straight down my spine to my balls. I was lucky I was alone, as I hadn't been guarding my thoughts very well. I tightened the walls around my mind as the elevator stopped on the ground floor.

Feeling safer in my thoughts, I returned to where I was. When this war was over—if it was over—would I have the courage to do it then? Would the three of us continue as we were, or would Corbin leave? There was no way I was leaving Angelina, so what about him? How did he feel? Was Corbin only in this because he didn't want to lose her? Or the power that he—we had? Or did he feel something more profound for Angelina—for me?

If I was honest with myself, I needed to admit I had feelings toward Corbin. Ones that I didn't quite understand, and I was wrestling with myself on how to handle them.

I went into the coffee shop on the main floor and found many more people milling around than I expected. We weren't set to leave for another couple of hours, but I guess I wasn't the only one dealing with anxiety at the battle to come.

After I got my coffee, I sat at one of the tables and turned on the virtual screen to see what was happening in the world. Everything seemed normal—almost as if none of these last several months had happened. In fact, there was little talk of torturing and killing any vampires.

Did they think that they had already massacred the majority of our breed? Were we fighting a losing battle? I hadn't been in this world long enough to know just how many breed members there were, but if we had over four thousand fighting with us, I had to believe there were many more than I initially thought.

A few minutes later, I felt Corbin enter the shop. My groin tightened again at his mere presence, and the thought of him under my body slammed into me. I shoved those thoughts into the closet in my mind and almost laughed as I did it. Into the closet—who would have thought I would have such thoughts?

I focused my attention on the screen before me, although I was acutely aware of Corbin's every move.

After he got his coffee, he approached. I watched through his eyes as he stared at my back, looking me up and down, and then he reached out to touch my shoulder. Even though I knew he was about to do it, his touch still startled me. It was like I had been watching a movie screen for a moment and it wasn't happening right there and then.

"Sorry," he said with a chuckle. "I figured you knew I was there."

"I did. Still surprised me, though." I flicked my wrist, closing the screen I had been staring at as I dwelled on what was coming.

He sipped from his coffee, observing me. "Can I ask you a question?"

"Shoot."

"What do you think of all this?"

I stared at him, blinking a few times. "Um, I think we have a good plan, and hopefully, it will work."

He cocked his head slightly, his green eyes staring hard. "That's not what I was talking about, and you know it, Hugh."

Maybe I did, but I wasn't going to admit it. "No, actually, I didn't." I shifted my cup around the table. "If you are talking about this thing with Angelina, I haven't given it much thought."

He chuckled huskily behind his mug. "Yeah, right, liar."

I sighed and leaned forward, lowering my voice, then said, "Fine, I have, but I don't know what you want me to say here."

"Honesty. Do you want me to back out of this once this mess is handled?"

I looked at him, slightly surprised. "Do you want to back out?"

He thought momentarily. "Look, I know you and Angelina have strong feelings for one another. While this has been fun and all, I'm not sure where I fit in."

I wanted to say, right there next to us, but I held back. "I think that might be up to Angelina to decide."

"I think it's up to you," he said pointedly. "If it were up to her, I'm pretty sure she'd like things to stay the way they are."

"What makes you say that?"

He laughed as he set his coffee on the table and leaned forward so he could also speak softly. "Lena loves the power, and she loves the sex. I'm not going to deny that I do, too." I watched his lips for a moment, suddenly wanting them wrapped around my cock. I tore my gaze away and back to his eyes as I shifted in my seat. "But I know you aren't in the same boat as the two of us. I don't want to come between what you two have. I guess that's what I'm saying. If you two decide that you'd rather I break the bond, I'll do that."

"But you would rather not?"

His gaze was direct, and I felt his honesty clearly. "Yes."

For a few seconds, we watched one another, and my emotions spun in turmoil. "I think Angelina and I will need to discuss it, but we keep things the way they are now."

"Yeah, for now, but eventually, we will have to discuss this and decide if we stay this way and figure things out—or not."

What would figuring these things out mean? Do we all live together? Do we share one big bed? Do we rotate with her—with each other? I had no fucking clue.

"Corbin"—I hesitated—"I'm not sure what I want." I stared at my cup, my mind returning to the images of him under me earlier.

Corbin pushed his hand across the table. His fingers barely

touched my hand, and I glanced around, but everyone seemed lost in their own worlds, not giving two shits about us.

"I saw what you were just thinking," Corbin said huskily, and I felt my cheeks begin to warm. "If that is what you want, then I'm yours. I do not doubt that Lena would love to watch, help, and be part of that."

I cleared my throat and shifted my hands away, sitting back in my chair. "See, I'm not sure how I feel about that."

"I told you before to stop overthinking it. There is nothing wrong with what you are thinking. You have to do what your mind, heart, and soul want. Don't fight your nature, Hugh."

"That's easy for you to say, but I haven't been in this world very long."

Corbin sighed, pulled his hand back, and then sipped his coffee. "How about we shelve this conversation and focus on current events first? Then we can all discuss it once we are back and things have calmed down."

His gaze was trained on the door. "Sounds like a plan," I replied as I felt Angelina walk into the café. Had he felt her before me? Had he said to table the discussion because she was approaching?

She joined us and put her hand on my shoulder. "How long have you two been down here?"

"Just a few minutes," Corbin stated with a smile, making me shift in my seat again. He glanced my way and gave me a knowing look.

"Has anyone seen my sister yet? We are supposed to leave in less than two hours."

"I haven't seen her," I answered.

At that moment, Joshua strolled in, and Angelina waved him over. "Where is Kris?"

"She and Zander are with Portage, going over last-minute plans."

She thanked him. "I'm going to go find them. One of you grab me coffee and bring it to me."

"Will do," Corbin replied as she hustled away distractedly. After she was gone, he looked at me with a smirk. "So, which of us is going to be the errand boy today?"

I chuckled as we both stood and moved to the counter together. "I think Lena has us both wrapped around her little finger."

"Pfft, she's got us wrapped around more than that." His words brought back my earlier thoughts, and I tried to push them away again, but when I glanced at Corbin, I knew he was aware of them.

The two of us took our coffee and hers and headed toward the elevator to take us up to the conference room, where I assumed everyone would be. The moment the door was closed, Corbin was in front of me, and I jerked the two cups out of the way before he crushed them against me. His chest pushed me back against the stainless steel of the box, and he wrapped his large hand around my neck and crushed his lips to mine.

His lips weren't the only thing pressing against me. His entire torso was plastered to mine, and once upon a time, I would have freaked out, but this was Corbin. I had already kissed him and sucked his cock. I tilted my head slightly and opened my mouth to accept his kiss. A few seconds after it started, he pulled back, glanced at the coffee cups in my hands as if just remembering them, and then smirked at me.

The elevator door began to open, and his light-green eyes nailed mine. "If that doesn't tell you what I want, I'm not sure any other words would."

Yeah, and my actions were speaking quite loudly themselves.

NOT LONG AFTER, we loaded into box trucks we were using to transport us and got on the move. Neither Corbin nor I had spoken since, but we had shared a few heated gazes. With the tension so thick around us, I didn't think anyone would notice. Angelina sure didn't.

While some whispered with the people beside them, most remained silent, contemplative, and anxious.

One thing that most people stressed over was that some of the breed was doing the strike with the sun high. There had been a short discussion of us attacking during daylight, but we wouldn't be able to

use the human-turned if we did that. They were critical for our plan—
at least on the east coast, so striking early was removed from the table.

On the other side of our transport, seven human-turned lay side
by side, deep in their sleeping trance. What would it be like to have
your mind completely shut down like that? I couldn't imagine not
having control of myself while I slept.

This was dangerous for us, driving toward our targets since the
human-turned couldn't provide us with shields. They would wake
shortly before we arrived and could hide us for the last few minutes,
but until then, we were sitting ducks.

The drive to Washington took just over four hours, and the closer
we got, the more the tension built. I could feel it in the bond I had
with Corbin and Angelina and Kristin and Zander, who were in
another transport going in the same direction a few miles ahead of us.

Kristin might be acting cool, but she was anything but. I'd felt her
thinking about our daughter quite often, and there was always an
anxious feeling associated with it. Was she worried for Briella's safety
or ours? She had assured me that Isaac would protect her, so I had to
assume it was something else. At one point, I saw a brief picture in her
mind. She was lying on the ground, pale and lifeless.

I ground my teeth. Was that what Kris was worried about? She
thought she would die in this raid and was picturing it? I wanted to
tell her to stop thinking so negatively, but just then, Angelina leaned
forward, looking around Corbin at me. I winked at her, and she
smiled.

"Please be careful," she whispered to me. "I just got you; I don't want to
lose you."

"Did you say the same thing to Corbin?" I asked her back, not in an
angry way, just curiously.

She chuckled into my head. "Something similar, I guess."

For a second, I didn't respond, and then I did. "Angelina, when this is
over, do you want the three of us to stay together?"

She hiked a brow. "You want to discuss that now?"

I shrugged. "I'm just wondering what you were thinking."

She hesitated only slightly before responding. "I think it is perfect *the way it is. However, I am sure Corbin would understand if that is not what you want."*

Corbin turned and looked me in the eye. I was well aware that he knew what we were discussing. I had felt him in my mind. As I returned his gaze, I replied to Angelina, *"I think I would like to keep things as they are. It feels right, the three of us."*

Corbin's gaze heated for a second, and then we both turned to Angelina. She looked like she had just won the lottery and squealed, *"I love you guys!"*

None of us had a chance to say anything else because the earpieces in our ears advised us that we were three minutes out. The three of us shared another look, and then we all seemed to withdraw into ourselves as we prepared ourselves mentally for the fight.

I dwelled on the image I had seen in Kristin's mind for a moment. She was nervous and worried about what was to come. I knew damn well that would never happen—not with all of us there to protect her.

I might not be mated to or in love with her anymore, but I did love her. I also knew how damn important she was to the breed, and like everyone else here, I would do anything to protect her.

CHAPTER SIX

JOSEPH

I wouldn't admit it to anyone, but I looked forward to this battle. Yes, I had partnered with Mistress Prissy Pants and her sex-crazed cohorts, but I only did it because they held the power I needed.

If I could have found a way to defeat the humans alone, I would have. Unfortunately, the world had gotten out of control. Whenever I sent people out to do my work, they almost always never returned. Stupid fucks were getting themselves caught.

I lost a lot of decent people because of that. I frowned as I stared at the shutters closed against the sun. I hoped that the next time they came down, things had changed.

I was golden as long as everything I had worked my ass off to set up earlier went off without a hitch.

"Sir, the mistress is here to see you," Adam spoke from the door, and I turned to him as I locked my mind down. I was so close. The last thing I needed was for her to see even a second of what was coming for her.

"Show her in." I cleared my throat and straightened my suit jacket. I would not fight today unless I had to, so there was no reason to wear any other clothing besides my business suit. I would be face-to-face with the president, so it seemed only fitting.

I stood beside my chair when Kristin and Zander stepped into the room. That chaffed my ass almost as much as her sister and her two mates. Two mates! Who would have thought that you could mate with two people? I had never heard of such a thing, but these fools had accomplished it.

I hated to admit it, but I was jealous of their power. When I first heard that they had done that, I immediately wondered how I could control them. Thoughts of compelling them to my side had rushed through my mind, but Angelina quickly told me that she could not be and could also break any compulsion put on others.

That irked me, but I wasn't about to give up. I had seen what they could do, and I was impressed. I wasn't impressed easily, either. I would find a way to get them to work with me. My one big question was, could Angelina tell if someone was compelled? I hoped not.

"Were you able to rest?" I asked as Kristin poured herself a cup of coffee from the carafe.

"Surprisingly, I did," she replied with a hint of a smile. She handed the coffee to Zander and then poured another one. Zander and I locked eyes, and I made sure my thoughts were locked up tightly. I didn't need him digging into my mind, either.

"Zander," I said and took a seat with my coffee.

"Joseph," he replied in a rough tone that did not hide his disdain for me. I ignored it as I had for the last few years. I should have known earlier that he would never stay by my side. His former Julian soul was too strong for me to control, and I should have driven a stake through his heart the moment I realized who he was.

"Are you ready for today?" Kristin asked as she sat opposite me and crossed her right leg over her knee. She wore black leather pants, a deep-purple silk shirt, and black boots that reached her knees, although they didn't have pointy high heels like her sister preferred to wear. I briefly wondered what Kristin would look like in a pair of fuck-me heels and nothing else, but when Zander glared at me, I dropped that train of thought.

"Indeed," I replied. "Are you as well?"

"Of course," she said in a bright voice that belied her tension. "Is everything in place?"

"Yes, I spoke with Gideon a few hours ago. He said everything was in place, and he had spoken to each target point, and they were all prepared to go."

"Yes, I spoke with him also." Kristin smiled, but in her eyes, I saw something that gave me pause. There was tension, but I didn't think it was for what was to come. That tension seemed directed toward me. I wasn't sure why I felt that, but I did. Had she somehow gotten into my mind? Had I not shielded myself well enough?

I cleared my throat. "That's good. Is there anything else you need to do before we leave?"

She bounced her leg for a moment, then glanced at Zander. "Do you mind giving us just a moment?"

His brows lowered. "Why?"

"Because I wish to speak with him privately. Go find my sister and make sure she is ready."

The two of them stared at one another for a moment, and then he nodded and left the room without a backward look.

I waited for her to speak, knowing she was listening for the elevator. I listened carefully too, and once I heard the doors close again, I cocked a brow and waited.

"If you think you will pull one over on Zander or me, you are wrong, Joseph. We only partnered with you on this endeavor because it was the best decision for our race. I suggest that you rethink whatever it is you have planned."

I laughed softly and looked around the room briefly before I stared her in the eye. "I don't know what you are talking about, Kristin. We are on the same side here."

"Are we?" Her leg stopped bouncing. "I'm not stupid, Joseph. While I don't know what you have planned, I know it will not turn out as you hope it will."

I shifted to the edge of my seat. "I have nothing planned that we have not spoken about, Kristin." I stood and stepped away. "And I'm rather disappointed that you would think I would have something up my sleeve."

I heard her stand, and I turned toward her. Having your back on your enemy was never good—especially when your enemy was a mated reborn with a vendetta. We might be working together today, but we were still enemies, and I wasn't stupid enough to forget that.

She stared at me, and I fought like hell to remain calm and keep my mind clear of thoughts.

"You aren't fooling me, Joseph. I don't know exactly how you plan to achieve your desired outcome, but it will not turn out as you hope."

"What outcome do you think I am wishing for?"

She lifted her chin. "Me being dead."

I scoffed. "Why would I want you dead? We are finally working together. I don't want to ruin that. I hope that after this fight, you and I might remain friends."

She laughed. "Friends? Joseph, we couldn't be friends if we were the last two vampires on this earth."

I frowned slightly. "Maybe it is you who has something planned. You are powerful, and I am no match for you. I am acutely aware of that. Why would I want to get on your bad side? I am hoping that we can work together. That we can build a better world for our breed."

She stepped closer just as I heard the elevator door open again and voices in the hallway. "I suggest you put a halt to whatever plans you have, Joseph. If you even remotely think there might be a chance for us to work together, then you will. I am telling you that whatever you have planned will not end as you wish." She stood a foot in front of me, her eyes a light silver. "Now that you know just how strong I am, how strong Zander, Lena, Corbin, and Hugh are, do you really want to piss any of us off?"

I didn't speak, but she didn't expect me to.

Her next set of words was said in a low voice that no one else outside of the room would have heard. "Change your plans, Joseph, or the death that will happen—will be your own, and it will come at my hand."

After Kristin had issued her threat—and that was precisely what it was—she had stepped away, changed her expression, and retook her seat, just as the door opened and Zander returned with Lena.

I tried not to think about what she said as Lena asked a few questions to ensure she had the timing correct. Zander remained quiet, watching my every move until I wanted to shout at him to stop.

I was unnerved by the mistress's ability to know something was up. How could she know? Did she see inside my head? There was no way. I had been so careful and never once felt her inside my mind. Was it possible for her to be there without me knowing? Had Zander gotten into my mind somehow?

It wasn't until they all left and descended in the elevator that I allowed myself to dwell on the issue.

There was no way she could know what I had planned. She had to be bluffing, perhaps expecting me to take advantage of her attention being elsewhere during the raid of the White House. That had to be it, and who was she to know what would or would not happen?

My goal was to regain control of our world, make the humans bow to us, and then pull the rug out from under her and Zander. The best way to do that would be to kill her. I knew it would be hard with all of them there, but I had a plan and knew it would work.

This time, once she was dead, I was going to do to her what I did to Alex. I would plunge a stake deep in her heart so there was no chance in hell that she would ever return.

CHAPTER SEVEN

ANGELINA

I was trying not to freak out about what we were about to do. I was no stranger to violence, but this was on a field I had never played before. I was used to dealing with justice for our kind.

Yes, many years ago, I had killed a lot of humans, but I hadn't done that since Kristin, and I had mended fences. Okay, fine, I had killed a few humans over the last couple of years, but I didn't do it because I wanted to. I did it to survive. Most of those had been in recent months.

Instead of pondering what we should do, I thought about the two men near me. Our triple mating had been unexpected, and I wasn't going to deny that I loved the power and the fact that I had two men with me almost all the time. I wondered if my sister was jealous of that. I didn't think she was.

From what I could see, she was very content with Zander at her side. I liked that she was happy. She deserved to be. I wanted her to have everything her heart desired, and with Zander here now, if something happened to Kristin, there was no question who would lead the breed. He was destined to oversee it.

Julian might have once turned it down and handed it to Alex, but I knew that Zander would not do that now. He knew just how important it all was. I could see him ruling over us for many years, and by the time he stepped down, Garrett would be well-trained and prepared to take over.

Not that any of that would happen. Kristin was too powerful to be hurt seriously, and too many people were there to protect her.

I spoke with Corbin and Hugh mentally for a few moments, and I was thrilled that Hugh admitted that he wanted the three of us to remain together. When this was over, we would have a hell of a celebration. I just wondered where that celebration would take place.

I would prefer not to return to Joseph's hotel, and thoughts of returning to the compound were about as thrilling as being under Portage's roof. What I really wanted was to return to our home in Philadelphia. Did it still exist?

Would we have to remain in hiding? Or would we show the humans we were a force to be reckoned with? As much as I hated to admit it, my sister was right, and we needed to ensure that we didn't slay all the humans we came across today. If we did, it would make us look bloodthirsty and vicious. We might be that way by nature, but we didn't need to promote it—not in this battle.

I listened to the final instructions as Kristin's vehicle reached its destination. We would be very close to her. Close enough that if she needed us, we could be at her side within seconds.

I reflected on something Zander had said to me moments before we left. Kristin hugged me and then walked away to speak with Clayton, who said he had important information for her. With her attention diverted, Zander slipped into my mind. *"Lena, make sure you are near her. Isaac gave me a warning and said Kristin will get hurt. We have to be there to help her if that happens."*

"That's not going to happen." I had laughed into his head, but the serious look on his face dried up my laughter.

"I believe in what he said."

"How could Isaac know?"

"It wasn't Isaac who knew. It was Briella. Isaac told me that Briella was worried about her mother because she would be hurt badly."

48

"How can an infant know such things?" I scoffed back at him.

He raised a brow. *"How did she know that her father was being tortured? There is a lot that we don't know about that child, but I need to believe her."*

"Okay. We will be near and help if and when she needs it, but I think Isaac was just overly careful."

"I hope so, Lena, but I'm afraid I believe him and think she does too."

"Wait! She knows she's going to be hurt?"

"I don't know. I don't think Isaac said anything to Kris. Just be ready." He turned away from me, shutting down our connection as Kristin came to his side and put her arm around him.

I watched them walk away, and then I put that conversation into the back of my mind. Now Zander's words filled my head, and I wished I had a way to speak with this Isaac guy and ask what would happen and when.

Our truck was coming to a stop when I looked at Corbin and Hugh. Would this be the end of what we had? Would the three of us make it out together?

I reached out to my sister and felt her tension. A moment later, an image of Kristin lying still and pale filled my mind, and my mouth flew open as the image vanished. "You guys must watch Kristin. Zander warned me that something was going to happen to her."

"Your sister is going to be fine," Hugh stated with a shake of his head. "She's one scary bitch."

"What do you know?" Corbin asked at the same time.

"I don't know specifics. Zander just told me to be on alert. We have to stay near her and protect her."

"What exactly did Zander say?" Corbin queried.

"Isaac warned him that she would be hurt."

"How the fuck does he know that?" Hugh snapped.

"Because your daughter told him," I growled in a low tone.

Hugh's eyes grew large as if he understood, and then he nodded once. "Fine, we will stick close to her."

We didn't have time to talk after that because the human-turned had woken up and were standing up, preparing to do what they were assigned to do.

"Be ready," my sister's voice slipped into my mind.

"You be careful, Kristin."

"I will be fine."

"But Zander—"

"What happens is what is meant to be, Lena. Thank you for everything you have done for me. I haven't ever said this to you very often, but I love you."

"Kris—" She blocked me before I could say anything further.

I growled, "Goddamn it!"

"What?" Corbin asked as he got off the floor of the box truck and crouched beside me.

I shook my head, feeling exasperated. Why did she always have to play the fucking martyr? "Nothing."

The irritation with my sister was good, as I felt my powers begin to bubble under the surface. Emotions were always helpful in getting the blood pumping.

"Get ready." Zander's voice filled my head, but not from a private conversation. This was said through our earpieces. Hugh closed his eyes and took a long deep breath, and Corbin squeezed my hand as he got to his feet and helped me up.

Amazingly, I could feel Kristin's power begin to spread as the door opened. Even though our human-turned had put a shield around us, I could see an almost eerie fog drifting over the ground as it moved over the humans all around us. As it touched each human, it froze them in their current position.

"Do you see the fog?" I asked softly.

"What fog?" Hugh asked, and Corbin looked at me funny. I shook my head. Perhaps I imagined it.

"Never mind," I stated and watched the light-blue fog continue from the front gates of the White House as they barreled over the well-manicured yards toward the impressive building.

Kristin's job was to freeze everyone in and around the building so we could enter. She wanted to get in there with the least amount of bloodshed to prove that first, she could, and second, we were not out for blood and death.

As I jumped down, I eyed the creepy sea of statues. It was like standing in a modern-day museum, and I wasn't the only one looking around in amazement.

Movement off to the left caught my attention, and I grabbed Corbin and Hugh's hands to pull them along as we moved toward Kristin, Zander, and our Portage, along with others, as they moved toward the gates to the White House.

Corbin used his power to blast the electrical locks of the gates, and then we hurried toward the building. It seemed so easy—almost too easy—and as we reached the doors, I wondered why we hadn't done this earlier.

Perhaps it was because we all didn't have the powers that we had now—duh! We moved at superspeed around the humans, not hurting them. Even though their bodies were frozen, they could move their eyes and see. When we moved slowly enough for them to see us, you could see the surprise in their features. It was almost comical.

We reached the room that we wanted in less than a minute. It had been so simple that I was almost disappointed—almost. Zander's warning was still buzzing around in my head, along with the picture of Kristin lying too damn still to be alive.

As soon as we reached the door, the human-turned with us began to work to put a barrier around the room to keep our presence hidden and ward off others who might break free of the compulsion and want to come in.

Kristin studied Zander for a moment, then nodded, and he pulled open the door. We all stepped in and looked around the room carefully. No matter where Kristin moved, Zander always stayed within arm's reach of her. Portage and Kristin moved around opposite sides of the room, looking over the computer screens and papers on the table. Kris shook her head several times, then pulled out an empty chair and took a seat. Zander stood directly behind her, and she crossed her legs and rested her hands in her lap before she said, "This room only, unfreeze."

The energy in the room amplified intensely as people began to move around, and some began to panic. Jett, Ryker, and Paxton stopped people who darted toward the doors. My eyes followed Kristin's as they scanned the room and landed on the president at the head of the table. At the other end of the table stood Portage.

The president's face was ashen, but he remained seated like most of the people.

"Before you all get in a tizzy, know that we are not here to hurt anyone," Kristin said firmly. "If you all remain levelheaded, my people will remain the same."

"How the hell did you get in here?" one man asked angrily.

Another one yelled, "She's going to kill us all." He closed his eyes as if he was praying.

Kristin did not respond; she merely kept her attention on the president.

"Perhaps the two of us could speak privately," the president said. He was in his sixties, an attractive man with gray hair and model-worthy facial features. Before all of this, I had liked him. I wasn't sure how I felt now.

"I believe that everyone in this room should be part of the discussion for the first part of this conversation. Especially since this weekly meeting is about my breed that you are discussing."

Heads turned to look between the two of them, and tension filled the room.

"Are you going to introduce yourself?" he asked her after he leaned back in his chair slightly as if to appear to be relaxed.

Kristin smiled and got to her feet slowly, causing many surrounding the table to shift as if preparing to run. Kris walked casually around the table toward the president, and two men moved toward him. He held his hand up to halt them just as Hugh moved to stop one, and Conner blocked the other. A few steps behind her was Zander, watching her like a hawk.

Kristin held her hand out to the president. "Sir, my name is Kristin Armstrong. I am known to my people, the vampire breed, as the mistress and ruler of our kind, at least here in the United States."

"Tom Kincaid." He took her hand and shook it. She released it after a firm shake and stepped back, glancing at Zander.

"You should also meet my mate, Zander Armstrong, the master of our race."

Zander stepped forward and shook his hand, and the president nodded. "Armstrong?"

"My father was Alexander Armstrong," Zander replied as he let go of the man's hand.

His eyes popped wide momentarily, then he frowned slightly. "I wasn't aware that he had more than one son."

"He has several," Zander replied.

"A topic of conversation for another time," Kristin said, then pointed to the other side of the table. "And that is Joseph Portage."

The two men nodded at one another, but neither spoke.

The president scanned the room, taking in all the rest of the vampires. "Perhaps one day you will introduce me to your friends." I winked at him as he looked me in the eye, and he shifted back noticeably as he tore his gaze from mine. Corbin chuckled by my side.

"Don't scare the guy," Corbin whispered into my mind with a laugh.

Kristin smiled again. "Perhaps I will when we have more time." She glanced at the man sitting to the president's right and hiked a brow. Her eyes were a bright blue right now. He jumped from his seat, and Kristin took it as soon as it was vacated.

"What is it that we need to discuss?" the president said as he retook his seat, glancing nervously at Zander as he stood between Kristin and him.

"There is no need to worry, Mr. President. Zander will not hurt you. No one here will hurt anyone—as long as they do not attempt to hurt us." She paused momentarily, then continued. "I wish to have a peaceful talk and settle a few matters."

He swallowed. "I will hold you to the peace talk. Now, what is it that you wish to discuss?"

Kristin glanced around the table, looking each one of them in the eye before she turned back to the president. I watched her eyes turn from bright blue to light silver as she did. Oh goodie! Things were about to get interesting.

"I want to know when you intend to stop imprisoning and killing my people because if you continue the way you are right now, the next people to die will be the ones sitting around this table."

CHAPTER EIGHT

KRISTIN

On the way to the location, I dwelled over the information that Clayton had given me moments before we left. Months ago, after Hugh had transitioned, I asked Clayton to start looking into our DNA. When we had to go underground, it was harder to take care of that, but eventually, he had been able to figure it out.

A human had forty-eight chromosomes. A vampire had forty-nine, and a reborn vampire had fifty. There was a way to tell if a human carried the reborn gene by doing a simple blood test.

That was not the news that surprised me today. Today, Clayton told me something much more helpful—if not imperative to know. The information filled my mind, and I wondered how to play this card best.

Only Clayton and Lainey knew about it, and if there were time to explain it all, I would have told Zander, but he would have to trust me.

When we arrived at the White House, everything started as planned. The instant the human-turned had shielded our group, the door had been thrown open, and I was right there with Zander at my side, helping me send out my command for them to freeze. A light-blue haze drifted from me and rolled over the ground, moving faster and faster as it gained speed. Every person it had touched stopped movement instantly.

Unfortunately, a few people in one of the other trucks jumped the gun and unloaded before it was safe. Two men in military garb opened fire, and three of ours went down. They would survive if they didn't bleed out.

Once the people on the front lawn of the White House were frozen, getting inside was easy—easier than I had anticipated, and it made the hackles on the back of my neck rise. Perhaps it was luck, but I wouldn't look a gift horse in the mouth for now. I knew what was coming.

Now I sat in the large conference room with charts, reports, and photographs of the violence done to my breed. The need to tear their heads from their bodies was strong, but I refrained—barely. It would not take much to knock me over the edge.

After the warning that I had received from my daughter, I knew that I needed to accomplish as much as possible in the short time that I had. Would I be able to do enough?

Briella's vision was short but gave me enough to know when and where it would occur. I had tried not to contemplate what would happen or how everyone would feel after it ended. The hardest part was knowing I would leave those I loved, including Zander and Briella. I had not had enough time with either of them, but my time was up. I was destined to always be on the fringes of happiness and never truly achieve it.

I had been careful not to share that information with Zander, although I knew he was on edge. He was hiding something, but I had enough to worry about without adding his stress to mine.

I scanned the room, taking in the thirty-odd people, plus my group, and noted the time was five-twenty-nine. I had forty-six minutes before this life ended.

I turned to the president. "I want to know when you intend to stop imprisoning and killing my people because if you continue the way you are right now, the next people to die will be the ones sitting around this table."

The room was silent for a moment, then three people at the other end of the table began to talk at once. I lifted my hand, pressing it in that direction. "Silence!" They stopped talking immediately, and the president's eyes enlarged before he cleared his throat and shifted his nervous blue eyes to me.

"I want to deny that I know what you are talking about, but I can't, Ms. Armstrong."

"Kristin."

He nodded and swallowed nervously. "Kristin." He took a deep breath and blew it out like he knew he had no choice. "Why did you not come to speak with me sooner? After the facility's destruction in Ohio, I expected you to appear on my doorstep."

"Were you aware of that facility?"

He cleared his throat nervously. "I was aware that one existed, but I honestly did not know what they were using it for."

"You knew one existed, but not what was happening inside? Were you aware that I was taken and held prisoner there?"

"Yes, I did receive word that you were there." He paused. "I am also aware that you and your people destroyed it and killed everyone working there when they freed you."

I stared at him. "But do you know what they were doing inside that building?"

"It was a research facility."

"Research?" I chuckled. "What kind of research were they doing, Tom?"

He looked slightly befuddled. "I'm not exactly sure. I was told that they were researching your species."

"Breed," I stated back to him.

He nodded as if to accept my term and glanced off to the side.

"Are you telling me that you were unaware they had an underground jail facility with over a thousand cells to hold my breed captive while denying us everything and treating us like animals by shocking us until we were incapacitated?"

His blue eyes widened, and he glanced to the side to look at a man sitting there. I followed his line of vision as Tom replied, "I was not aware of that."

I glanced at Cameron, who nodded to me. Thanks to Cameron, I would know if he was being truthful.

"The president wasn't involved in that." The man Tom had looked at spoke up as he shifted slightly in his seat.

"Why is that, Aaron Spellman?"

His brown eyes widened. "How do you know my name?"

"I not only know your name but your wife's name and where both of your children attend college." I glanced around the table. "I know all your personal information."

My eyes landed on a woman sitting at the other end of the table. Unlike everyone else, she didn't seem afraid of us. I saw the intrigue in her eyes as she studied me back, which was good.

She was also a pretty woman; I could tell she would be strong and helpful to our future. He would like her, well, hopefully, he would like her.

I reached out to my mate. *"Zander, Michelle Becker is a reborn. She is unaware of it, but please make sure she is removed from this room and returned to the compound."*

"How the hell do you know that?"

"When this is over, speak with Clayton."

The room was silent after the bombshell I had dropped. Many people looked around, and some fidgeted in their seats. "I have quite a few people who enjoy research—the nonviolent kind—so they completed a background file on every one of you. It was quite an impressive read." I paused and looked back at the guy I had been talking to. His red tie was slightly skewed as if it had been a long day. "Aaron, I believe you were going to tell me why Tom wasn't made aware of the facility and what you were doing."

"He is a busy man. He didn't need to know what we were doing."

I smiled at him, showing him the tips of my fangs. "Plausible deniability, huh?"

His voice cracked as he began, "We only wanted to understand you."

I laughed. "Understand us? Aaron, you were imprisoning members of my breed with special abilities."

"Yes." He cleared his throat. "We were. I won't deny that, but you didn't have to kill all the humans there."

I cocked my head. "But I didn't."

"Well, your people did."

"My people were furious that they had been taken prisoner and treated like animals. You shocked them repeatedly until they were unconscious and made them wear shock collars so you could control them. What the hell do you think they would do when they got free? I never once gave the order to take that building down. They did that independently, and I'm glad they did." I stared at him for a few seconds. "Do you have any more facilities like that?"

He looked down. "No."

I dug into Aaron's head and saw him telling himself not to mention the new facility in Georgia that they had just opened.

I told Hugh, *"They are building a new facility in Georgia. You are tasked to free anyone there and destroy the building. This time don't kill all the humans."*

"You got it," he replied, rolling his shoulders back as if proud to be given a task.

To Aaron, I said, "Let me have your word that you will never allow one of those facilities ever to be raised again."

"I think we learned our lesson," Aaron said as he glared at me. I knew he was lying, but he would be dealt with accordingly later.

"Perhaps," I commented back, giving him a knowing smile. "But I doubt it."

The president cleared his throat. "What exactly do you want to accomplish here, Kristin?"

I studied him and his serious light-blue eyes. "I want a truce. I want you to stop killing my people. I also want you to stop treating them like criminals and locking them up to experiment with them."

"Aaron already said that we weren't doing that anymore."

"Well, you must excuse me as I do not believe him, and you shouldn't either." I glanced to the end of the table; Portage held my gaze for a moment. I still hadn't figured out how he would do it, but I knew he would be behind what was to happen to me today.

I shifted back to the president. "I remember when military forces could not operate on American soil, but now you have your military hunting and slaying my people within the country's borders. Why? Why have you called for war with my people? We have done nothing to the humans as you did to my people. It's like what was done to the American Indians all over again."

"I'm afraid that when you blew up that facility, it was seen as an act of terrorism."

"So, you blame an entire race for something a few did? What happened to equality? Is that not the same as when the World Trade Towers were bombed in 2001 with planes, and the entire world hated anyone Muslim? Or when the pandemic happened in 2020, and everyone blamed the Chinese? Until a couple of years ago, you never even knew we existed. We have been living amongst you all for thousands of years, and…" I paused and turned to glare at Joseph. "And because someone had to open their mouth and make it public, everyone automatically assumed we were all killers and evil—which we are not. We live a rather peaceful existence."

"Equality?" Aaron butted in. "But I seem to recall you said to members of our task force that you were your own entity and that your race was not subject to the laws of humans."

"I did say that." I nodded. "But that was in the case of protecting and punishing our own. Your representatives were there to obtain a list of people with abilities to detain and abuse them."

"That is not true," he stated.

Hugh stepped forward. "That is precisely true, Aaron. I should know since I was the one asking for the information."

"Who are you?" he asked, looking Hugh up and down.

"Hugh McMurphy. I oversaw the task force in Philadelphia."

"But you're one of them," he stated, slightly horrified.

"Yes, I am," Hugh replied proudly.

"So you sold your soul to the devil," the man beside Aaron hissed.

Hugh chuckled. "Not at all. I was one of them. I just didn't know it."

The president sighed wearily. "Obviously, there is a lot that I need to be brought up to speed on."

"I thought that was the purpose for these meetings," I stated.

He sighed. "I don't like what has been happening any more than you do, Kristin."

"Then you will put a stop to it, right?"

He glanced around the table. "I'm not sure I can."

I laughed. "Of course, you can, Tom. You are the president of the United States. The commander in chief and you control the military forces. You can stop this, and I expect you to do just that."

"And if I am not able to do that?"

"Then you and everyone in here are dead," I stated plainly, without emotion, and he stared at me for a long time.

"You can't come here and threaten to kill us all."

"I can, and I have. Right now, I control your facility and everyone within these walls. If you look out the door, you will see a hallway full of people frozen in place. Do you know how easy it would be for me to have my people slay every one of them, drain them dry, and then walk away?"

"You wouldn't."

"I will be honest with you, Tom. I don't want to. That is not the kind of ruler that I am. Not the type of person that I am. I do not know if you are aware, but many years ago, I was a police officer, and I swore an oath to protect and serve. Over the years, I have continued to do that—of course, not with the humans as a police officer, but as the mistress of our breed. I protect our people, just like you protect the American human people."

"I was not aware of that."

"I am sure there is a lot you are not aware of." I glanced at the clock and saw that twenty minutes had passed. "If I had the time, we could have a nice long conversation and get to know one another better. Unfortunately, time is short, and at present, fifteen of your government facilities are fighting for their lives."

"What are you talking about?"

"I'm talking about the fact that I have people across the nation taking hold of your strongest government and military facilities. You wanted a war and started it, but the two of us can stop it if we work together." I paused and gave him a moment to think. "Are you ready to put a stop to this, Tom? I will stop my people if you say you are, and I believe what you say."

Tom glanced around the table, then looked at the people around the room. Finally, he looked at Aaron, and Aaron nodded solemnly to him.

"Kristin, I will end the war, but you must stop your people right now from hurting anyone else."

"Advise them to stop," I told Joshua, who stood near the door. He nodded and grew thoughtful, and I knew he was speaking to someone mentally outside the building.

"Done," he stated a moment later.

I turned back to the president. "My people have stopped or will within a few moments."

"How did he stop people? He didn't even say anything."

"He spoke to someone outside mentally. We can do that."

"There is a lot that we do not know about you."

I glanced at Zander and smiled sadly. "I know, and Zander will help you to understand our world." I wish that I could have been the one to work with the president, but the moments of my life were slowly counting down. I glanced at the clock; another six minutes had passed. Only twenty minutes left, and I still had a lot to accomplish.

CHAPTER NINE

ZANDER

Things were going well. Isaac's warning was wrong. Perhaps if things hadn't worked out as well as they did when we arrived, her life would have been in jeopardy, but things were calm. The president seemed willing to stop the war against our people.

I found it odd that Kristin wanted me to work with the president. I would have expected that to be on her list to handle. Perhaps she trusted me more than I thought. I was proud of my mate and swore I would never disappoint her. She was a powerful and intelligent woman who handled this tension-filled situation well. She kept her calm but was fierce enough to tell them she meant business. They might not realize this, but she had spared a lot of people today from needless violence. Both humans and our breed—if the humans stuck to their words.

Portage hadn't liked the idea when Kristin first devised the plan, but he was willing to be coerced when Kristin told him it was either her way or the highway. I glanced to the other side of the room. Portage watched Kristin leaning against the wall with his arms crossed over his chest as if he didn't have a care in the world. Fucking asshole.

I turned my attention back to my mate and the conversation they had just agreed on. Tom smiled kindly at Kristin. "Perhaps it's time for us to speak in private while my people start to put an end to this horror."

Kristin seemed tense as she stood, but her smile radiated warmth and confidence. "Perhaps it is time. I believe there is a lot for us to discuss." She glanced toward the wall, or was she eyeing Portage as I had?

The president relaxed even more. "Why don't we go to my private office? We can toast to a new world. God knows I could use a drink."

Kristin stared at him for a long moment and then nodded before reaching for my hand and squeezing it momentarily. "A new world would be wonderful. Zander, if you will excuse us. This conversation needs to be just the two of us for now. Please assist them with anything that they might need."

Tom glanced over his shoulder. "I can't go anywhere without my secret service."

"Do you honestly think that I would do anything to hurt you right now, Tom? I have spared a thousand lives today to accomplish this. The last thing I want to do is ruin that now. I respect you and wish you no harm."

Tom gave her an abrupt nod, looked over her shoulder, then brightened his smile as he extended his hand for her to proceed.

Suddenly a flare of something struck my body, but it was gone as fast as it arrived. Had that been fear? Pain? *"Kristin, I should go with you."*

She shifted to stare into my face, her eyes bright and full of love. *"There is no need, and I prefer that you stay here and help these people. Find out what else there is to know so you can take it back and plan for rebuilding our breed. I need you to ensure they call off the violence against our people."*

"Okay, then take Joshua, Hugh, or Corbin with you."

She turned and took both my hands. *"I'll be fine, Zander. Trust me, please. I must do this alone. I love you."*

As she let my hands go, I wanted to throw my arms around her and hold her to me forever. There was more to her words than she was letting on. If I wasn't mistaken, her hands had shaken slightly in mine. Before I could say anything else, she walked away with the president through a side door, saying that mated couples do not like to be apart and that she needed to calm my insecurities.

I stared at the door and frowned. Every fiber of my being urged me to go after Kristin, but I had to trust her. The entire compound was frozen, and she would be safe. She could take care of herself.

"All right," I said as I again faced the room. "Where do we start to get this done? I want the violence to stop immediately."

People spoke in a rush for the next few minutes, and the phone calls started. Orders were given, and information was passed to Angelina, Hugh, Corbin, Cameron, or me. With each minute away from Kristin, I began to feel increasingly on edge. That feeling only intensified when I glanced around the room and noticed Portage was no longer there.

"Where the fuck is Portage?" I asked Joshua who was closest to me.

Joshua shrugged. "He said he was bored and going to head back to his place."

"Goddamn it!" I growled and rushed past Josh toward the door where Kristin had departed. I was only two feet outside the meeting room when I felt something deep inside me explode through my gut.

A feeling of fury and pain nailed me so intensely that it almost took me to my knees. The only thing that kept me on my feet was knowing it was coming from Kristin. Even though the victory was almost ours, our enemy had found a way to attack our most vital link.

A fraction of a second later, I gathered myself and rushed down the hallway toward a door where I could feel her. Just as I reached the door and yanked it open, a sound that I had never heard—and would never forget—tore through the air and stopped me in my tracks.

Kristin was on the far side of the room, seven men circling her, and all of them had electrical blasters pointed and firing in her direction—all seven at the same fucking time. With everything she had done today and all the power she had used, she was no match for the seven lines of electrical charge. Her face was directed toward the ceiling as she let loose an animalistic sound somewhere between a feral growl and a wounded animal. Her arms were out at her sides as if nailed to a cross. Her back arched to the furthest extent, and her body radiated an unnatural yellow glow.

From the corner of my eye, I saw someone flee the room. Portage! On the other side of the room stood the president, looking horrified at the scene before him.

To the depths of my soul, I felt Kristin's pain so intensely that I couldn't move my feet. They were cemented to the floor as I watched the life draining from her. The electricity continued battering her for another two seconds, and she dropped her chin and peeled open her eyes. They landed on mine, and I saw the scariest thing I had ever seen in them. Gone was her glorious and infamous glowing silver. In its place was the black of night. Almost as if her eyes had been plucked from her skull.

Her voice filtered weakly into my mind and chilled my soul as it echoed inside me. *"Briella foresaw this. You must accept my fate."*

How the fuck could Briella have seen this? Why would she show Kristin this scene? I opened my mouth and screamed in a voice I did not recognize as my own, "No!"

I threw my hands out with the words. All seven men were lifted off their feet and flew through the air to slam against the wall. The electrical blasts were disengaged, and Kristin crumpled to the ground just as someone else rounded the corner. I somehow knew it was Corbin without looking. I focused on getting to Kristin and slid across the floor to her side just as her head bounced off the floor for the last time.

A scurry of movement was around me. There were violent screams of anguish as our sentinels attacked the men, pleas for their lives, and then silence. The sounds mixed with flashes of memories from my life with Kristin.

The first night I saw her at Night Crawlers—the smile on her face as she sat beside me in my Mustang, letting her hand fly in the breeze out the window. The first taste of her blood as I took her vein in the driveway of the VMF house. The feeling of our bodies becoming one as our mating began.

The images passed so quickly as I lifted Kristin into my arms. Suddenly, another scene flashed through my mind. My son, Damon, sliced her throat and threw her to the ground before he rushed into the night. He had broken my soul that night, and it had not mended for over thirty years when I ran into Officer Kristin Greene on a dark road in Fawn Hollow Township.

"Kristin! Kristin! Wake up! Baby, you have to wake up! Please! Oh my god! Kristin, this is not over! Do not leave me! This is not the end of our story!" I felt for her pulse, closing my eyes and blocking out every other sound so I could focus on her heartbeat. Thud-thump. There was one, then another a second later, and then a third a few seconds later, and that was it.

"Kristin! No! Goddamn it! You come back to me! You can't leave me! Kristin! Don't you do this! You promised me you would be okay. You swore you would be okay!" I screamed at her face, shaking her slightly as my eyes blurred with unshed tears, and I felt the tear deep in my soul of a mate being torn away from me.

I threw back my head and let loose an animalistic wail caused by the intensity of the pain.

"Zander," Corbin's voice broke through my hysteria. His hand landed on my arm. "Zander, she's gone."

"No!" I roared. "She can't be gone! She can't! I just found her again. It was our time! Goddamn it! It was our fucking time!"

Suddenly, a sweet, soft voice slipped into my mind like a jolt of lightning. *"She needs all of you."*

What. The. Actual. Fuck? I blinked, and then Isaac's words slammed back into my mind. "Get every reborn here! Now! We need all of them. Put your hands on her, Corbin! Now, goddamn it!" He stood beside me, and I reached up and yanked him to his knees. He stared at me as if I had lost my mind but put his hands on Kristin.

A few seconds later, Angelina was on the floor across from her sister, almost as emotionally wrecked as I was. "Zander, what the fuck happened?"

"It doesn't fucking matter what happened. We have to all work together to save her."

"Zander, her heart is not beating," Angelina said in a low voice as she stared at her sister's face.

"I know it's not, Lena! We have to help her."

"She's gone, Zander," Corbin said as I felt others join us, but I didn't care about any of them.

"Isaac told me it would take all the reborns to save her! Now every single one of you put your fucking hands on her!" I shouted as I glanced around at all the wide eyes staring at Kristin's lifeless body. "Now! What are you standing there for?"

Angelina shook her head as tears slipped from her eyes. "It's too late, Zander."

Hugh's voice barked over my head. "The fuck it is! Put your hands on her, Angelina! All of you down on the floor and touch Kristin. Push every ounce of power you have in your body toward her." He dropped beside me; I had never been so happy to have Hugh there. "You can heal, Angelina! Heal your sister! Bring her back. You have every single one of us to help you. You have all our power! Heal her! You can't let her die. Briella needs her. We all need her."

Angelina swallowed and then slowly put her shaking hands on her sister. She closed her eyes as hands suddenly came from every direction—not just the reborns, but the sentinels and others who had joined us. Angelina's power surged through her sister, and she began to glow. With all of us there focusing our energy on Angelina, I stared at Kristin's face, watching for any sign of life.

Angelina cried as her eyes opened and tears shimmered. "Her body is fried! I can't do this!"

"Lena, do not let your sister go. Focus on what needs to be fixed. Focus on her heart and her mind. Then we can repair the rest later. You can do this; I know you can." Hugh spoke firmly but softly toward her, and she nodded once and closed her eyes again.

Her power surged again, and I felt her directing it toward Kristin's chest. The glow around her pulsed and began to converge in her chest. It moved around her torso like someone was shining a flashlight through her translucent skin.

"Keep going, Lena. You got this," Hugh encouraged her. "You're doing great."

She worked for another thirty seconds, and then I felt a sudden surge of power blast into her chest, and Kristin's torso came off the floor. Her eyes flew open, and she gasped a loud breath. Her eyes closed again as her torso landed back on the ground, but this time, I heard her heart beating slowly. Way too slowly.

"She needs your blood," Lena said. "She needs a lot of blood. All of us will need to feed her to keep her healing."

I glanced at Lena as she started to topple to the side. Corbin caught her. "I got her. She's okay, just exhausted."

Hugh grabbed Kristin's hand and put his other hand on my arm. "We have to get her home to the compound."

"She needs to rest."

"Zander, we have to get her back to the compound. It's the only way she will live."

"How do you know that?"

"My daughter just told me that, and I believe her."

Had Briella reached out to him as she had me? Had she reached out to me, or did I imagine it? My mind was in disarray, and I nodded, and then Hugh picked Kristin up and put her into my arms. "Lead the way," I croaked in a rough voice as I held her tightly to my chest.

CHAPTER TEN

CORBIN

I hadn't thought much about Portage leaving the room. To be honest, I didn't know the man well, and I didn't like him, so what he did was of no concern to me.

However, it was a massive concern to Zander as he flew out of the room. A second later, there was no way we couldn't hear the anguished scream barrelling down the hallway. Even the humans heard it, and they all looked alarmed. Then Zander's single-word cry came from that direction, and I was the first one out the door, racing in his direction.

Seeing Zander on the floor holding Kristin to his chest was like a gut punch. Off to the side, the president watched, his face white as a sheet, and along the wall were seven human men crumpled to the floor. A few were starting to move around, but several weren't moving. Some of Kristin's people dealt with the humans, but my focus went to my brother and his mate.

I dropped to my knees beside Zander, my heart breaking for the incredible woman in front of me whom I had only just met. She was beautiful inside and out, and I could not imagine how badly he was hurting now.

He demanded that we all put our hands on Kristin, but what good would that do? She was gone. Only Hugh talked to everyone as if he believed Zander was correct and said something about his daughter telling him to do this.

I was so confused by that, but I did what they requested. If there was a way for Kristin to survive, it was through Angelina—but was it too late?

I pushed every ounce of energy I had toward Kristin for Angelina to use, along with everyone else. A tear dripped onto Kristin's body from Zander, but no one said anything as Angelina strained to direct the power through her sister's body. Sweat popped out on her brow as she worked harder than I had previously seen her.

What she was doing was incredible, and I was amazed by her abilities. Once Kristin gasped, and her heart beat softly, Angelina collapsed to the side, and I caught her.

Zander had Kristin in his arms, and Hugh was right by his side as they rushed from the room.

I lifted Angelina into my arms and turned toward the president. Cameron stood beside him, holding his arm as if keeping the man from fleeing. The president shook his head, his eyes pleading. "I didn't have anything to do with that. I swear. It was Joseph Portage. I saw the whole thing."

I glanced at Cameron. "He speaks the truth. You take care of Kristin and Angelina. Clayton, Henry, and I will deal with this."

"Deal with this?" the president said as he looked nervously toward Cameron. I didn't have time to stand there and see how that played out. I gave an abrupt nod and rushed out the door to find people moving around everywhere, alarm in their voices and movements.

When Kristin went down, their compulsion had vanished, and now they were all trying to figure out if they were under attack. I was out the door before anyone could stop me, with Angelina cradled in my arms. She held me as tightly as she could around my neck, and I felt how exhausted she was.

I had a close call with two guards who spotted me as I paused outside the building to get my bearings, but I was able to avoid their firepower and make it to safety.

I jumped into the back of the truck right before the door was closed, and I hadn't even set Angelina down before it was moving. About a dozen people were inside—some were sentinels, and a few were human-turned. Their attention focused on the other end of the box truck where Kristin lay in Zander's arms. Her dark-red hair was such a contrast against her pale, slack features. I listened closely for a moment and heard the faint beat of her heart. Hugh stood over them, looking down at the mistress with guarded features.

I led Angelina over to her sister and sat on the opposite side next to my brother. Angelina was staring at her sister's face, tears running down her cheeks.

"What happened?" she asked in a forlorn voice.

"Fucking Portage happened," Zander growled. "When I find that man, I will tear his limbs from his body one by one before I stake his fucking black heart."

"I'll hold him down while you do," Lena said, glancing up at me. I had a feeling there wouldn't be any shortage of people who wanted to help.

Hugh paced back and forth within the box truck. His hands fisted for a few minutes before he would splay his fingers and then clench them again.

"Hugh, take it down a notch," I told him.

His face snapped toward mine. "Take it down a notch? What the fuck! Portage just killed Kristin! I will not take it down a notch! We need to go find that motherfucker!"

"No, we need to stay with my sister," Lena replied in a low tone. "She might need us all again."

"What exactly happened in there? Did you see it?" Hugh asked Zander.

"Seven men were striking her with those strong electrical weapons. She lifted right off the ground as if she were floating, and her body glowed this eerie yellow," Zander said without emotion in his voice. "I saw that spineless dick run from the room and somehow stopped the men, but it was too late."

"We need to find him," Hugh growled.

"We need to take care of Kristin first," Lena stated firmly.

Zander's voice was soft as he spoke again. "She knew this would happen. She said she had seen it, and it was her fate."

"When did she say that?" I asked as Lena, Hugh, and I exchanged glances.

"As it was happening. It was the last thing Kris said to me." He brushed a hand over her face. "Kris, wake up, honey. That was not your fate. I'm your fate."

I looked at Hugh. "You said your daughter told you what to do?"

"Yeah, as fucking weird as it sounds, she told me we all had to work together and bring her home."

"Isaac warned me about this," Zander said.

Angelina exploded. "You fucking knew about this, Zander! You knew she was going to be hurt! Why didn't you stop her from coming?"

He lifted his face and glared at Lena. "Do you think she would have stayed at the compound if I told her to do so? Come on, Angelina. You know your sister as well as I do. There is no way she would have remained there."

"You told me earlier to keep a close eye on her! Why didn't you go with her when she left the room? You could have stopped him! You should never have let her go."

"She told me she had to speak with the president alone. How could I tell her no?"

"You could have tried to talk sense into her!"

He shook his head. "No. Isaac said she would be badly hurt, and we would need all of us to bring her back."

"How the hell did he know that?" she snarled sarcastically.

"Because of Briella," Hugh answered, and her face snapped to his. "She saw it, and I'm sure she gave Isaac a warning to give to Zander."

"But if Kristin knew this would happen, why did she come?"

Zander replied, "Maybe Briella told her she had to do this to protect the rest of us. You know as well as I do that Kristin would never put herself before others. She said this was her fate."

"Her fate is to live! Not die!"

Zander hissed at her, "She's not going to die! I'm not going to let her!"

Angelina raised her hand and replied tartly, "Zander, she already did." She paused momentarily, and her voice was softer as she continued. "I did everything I could, but it might not have been enough. I have no clue what I was doing! We don't know how she will come out of this or if she even will! I might have fried her brain or not repaired her right. She might be a vegetable. She would never want to be alive if that was her life. Maybe I shouldn't have tried to save her."

"Don't! Don't think like that. She's going to make it, Angelina. She can't die. I won't let her!" Zander hissed as he stared into her face and held Kristin tighter. He bit into his wrist and held it over her mouth, but she didn't attempt to drink. He let the blood drip into her mouth and then bit into his wrist repeatedly, every time it healed to keep the blood flowing down her throat.

I felt his energy waning. "That's enough, Zander. Let your blood work for a few minutes. Then one of us can feed her more."

He nodded and closed his eyes, leaning against the wall as the truck raced down the roadway. His arms wrapped tightly around Kristin as her head rested against his chest. The rest of us looked at each other without saying a word. I hoped Kristin survived, but I had to agree with Angelina. We didn't know if she would live or what she would be like once she woke up—if she ever did.

It took us almost six hours to arrive at the mountain compound. During that time, each of us took turns feeding Kristin. She was still unconscious, but her coloring had improved—slightly.

There were also seven of her guards in the back of the truck with us. They had remained quiet for most of it. Although a few had offered their veins to us to recharge. We thanked them but did not take them up on their offer.

During the downtime, I spent a lot of time thinking. My mind spun from one thing to another, constantly jumping. I dwelled over what happened tonight, over what the compound would be like. It switched gears, and I worried about Angelina and Hugh, and then I worried more for Kristin and Zander.

I eyed Zander closely. I hadn't known he was my brother until recently, but in just days—weeks—I had a strong bond with him. I felt his pain as if it were my own.

As the truck finally came to a stop, the back gate opened, and I helped Angelina to her feet. She had regained some of her strength, but not all of it.

Paxton had called ahead and advised them that we were inbound with Kristin. The moment the door was open, a hulking man was there, and I hoped like hell that he was on our side.

"Master." He reached for Kristin immediately, and Zander lovingly handed Kristin down to him. "I am glad that you listened to me."

"Is she going to live?" Zander asked as they rushed away, and Hugh, Angelina, and I followed closely on their heels.

I didn't bother to look around and take in my surroundings. There would be time for that.

"That depends on her," Isaac said. "She has things to do, but Briella has seen both outcomes."

"What?" Zander stopped in his tracks, and Hugh almost plowed over him as two other men rushed around the corner.

"What the hell happened?" one of them growled as they reached Kristin. Isaac turned on him and snarled enough to make the man back up a few steps.

"Calm the hell down, Isaac. She is our mother. We have the right to be worried about her."

"Rex, she's bad," Angelina said, touching his arm. "Gather the elders, and we will explain what happened after we get her settled and feed her again."

The younger man, who was not turned yet, studied his mother with concern and lifted his eyes to mine. His eyes appeared slightly haunted by something—guilt? He blinked, and the look disappeared as he stepped forward. "You must be Corbin. I'm Garrett, your other half brother."

Isaac started marching up the steps with Zander and Hugh on his heels. "I look forward to getting to know you, Garrett."

"Same," he said and stepped back, turning to watch Isaac, Zander, Hugh, and Kristin disappear around a corner. I rushed after them with Angelina at my side.

We followed them down a long hallway to the door at the end, and Zander opened it to allow Isaac entry. He carried Kristin straight through the room and to another hallway. I paused in the living room area where Hugh stared at someone off to the side.

I looked around him to see a woman holding a baby, and Hugh stepped forward and immediately took the child out of her hands. "Hello, Briella. It's nice to meet you finally."

The infant let out a coo that made Hugh smile, and she touched his face. He gasped and smiled down at her as tears began slipping down his face.

For the first time since Kristin went down, Angelina's features softened. She smiled slightly before walking toward the hall where Zander and Isaac had disappeared. I followed, wanting to give Hugh a few minutes with his daughter. Since we were mated, did that make the child my stepchild of sorts?

Inside a bedroom, Kristin was lying on the bed, her long red hair twisted off to the side and out of the way so Zander could lie beside her.

"What now?" I asked as I stood at the foot of the bed.

"Now," Isaac said as he looked my way, "we wait."

"For what?" Angelina asked.

"For the mistress to do what she needs to do."

"What the hell does that mean?" Angelina growled crankily as she crossed her arms over her chest.

"Briella told me that her mother has things to do before she can return to us if that is her choice."

"What?" Zander snapped. "What the hell does she have to do?"

"I do not know, Master. I only know that she has things to do." I heard someone enter the room behind me and saw Hugh holding his daughter.

"Briella wants to see her mom," Hugh said as he moved around us to the bed. He leaned down and set the child against Kristin's side. Briella looked over her mother as if checking to ensure she was whole and then wiggled closer to her. She closed her eyes and seemed to drift asleep in a heartbeat.

Isaac spoke softly, "We should leave them."

"I'm not leaving her," Zander said a bit louder.

"You can stay, but we should give them room. Kristin is healing, but she is also dealing with things. Briella will guide her."

"How is that child going to guide her mother?" I asked, utterly confused.

"Briella is speaking with her now. We must go and give them peace. It will be easier for her to speak with her mother and help her."

Angelina looked at me doubtfully. "Fine. We need to speak with the elders and explain what happened. You will come to get us if something happens."

He nodded, and we left Zander, Briella, and Kristin alone. I was so damned confused about how this child could be doing anything—especially talking to her mother.

CHAPTER ELEVEN

KRISTIN

We accomplished a lot in my brief few minutes with the president. Well, hopefully, we did. He would stop the hunting of the breed and work on a relationship with us to help the human citizens learn to accept us and not fear us.

I hoped that after things settled down, Zander could take over, and life for our people would improve.

Perhaps after turning the reborn, Michelle, Zander would take her as a mate. He needed someone at his side. I hated the thought of him being with someone else but also detested the idea of him alone.

I glanced at the clock. Only two minutes to go. If I fled from this room now, would my life be spared? Had I received that warning from my daughter to stop it? Part of me wanted to believe that, but the other part felt it was all meant to be this way.

If I were honest with myself, I was exhausted and tired of the constant stress of having to watch out for everyone—of proving myself constantly and dealing with drama. How had Alex done it for so long? Would it be better to die?

If I did, I would be leaving Zander. Maybe we were wrong and it wasn't our time. Perhaps I could return, and we would find each other again. He would control the breed, and I could work at his side rather than be in charge as I was now.

I didn't want to leave him, but what could I do? I needed to accept the inevitable—but how did you look on your upcoming death with acceptance? I had so much more to do and accomplish.

I was pretty sure that Briella would grow up to be an incredible woman and Hugh would be there to care for her. Lena, Corbin, and Isaac too. They would all survive my death. Like I had survived losing Trent, Julian, and Alex, they would grieve and then move on.

My only prayer was that I would not be staked so that I could come back. I could find them again. Now that we knew how to find reborns, they could search for me and prepare me for my future.

There were three doors in the room, and they opened simultaneously. I burst to my feet, preparing to fight as every instinct demanded, but when I saw the blasters, I knew I could not win. Eight men poured into the room, three blasters struck me immediately, and four more followed.

The pain was excruciating—worse than anything I had ever experienced before. No nerve in my body wasn't searing with pain, and as much as I wished I could hold back the sound, I knew I could not.

Zander was there before it was over, and I wished I could have kept him from seeing this, but just as I had witnessed the death of Julian, he was here to witness my final moments. He would enact vengeance on the eighth man in the room. I knew he had been up to something; I just hadn't known what or how. His mind had been locked down tightly all day.

It didn't matter now. This was my fate, and I focused on Zander for one brief moment and told him that. This was meant to be. I would accept my death gracefully.

Perhaps it wouldn't be so bad. When the pain stopped, I felt my body begin to float. I could still hear things around me but couldn't understand the sounds. Darkness filled my mind, and the sounds inside my body and around me slowly faded.

I wasn't sure how long it was; it seemed mere seconds before a bright light began to cast over me, and I wanted to shield myself from it. I didn't want to burn to death, but I found it didn't hurt as the light grew brighter. I lifted my face to the light, smiling as I inhaled the sweet scent of grass and listened to the soft sound of lapping water as it reached my ears. Birds chirped, and in the distance, I heard a bark.

The bark sounded again, and it was closer this time. Recognition burst through my mind, and I turned to find Garda, my Shiloh Shepherd from over thirty-five years ago, running toward me. His caramel-colored eyes were bright and happy as he raced in my direction. I dropped to my knees, throwing open my arms. "Garda!"

Tears instantly blurred my vision as he threw himself into my hold and began to wiggle and lick at my face. "I missed you so much! You have no idea how much I missed you. Every single day I thought about you!"

He sat back, his mouth wide open, his eyes shining as he stared at me with so much love. I pet his soft fur and then buried my face into his neck a moment before I heard a chuckle behind me.

I spun on my knees, preparing to attack someone behind me, but I froze when I found a man I never expected to see again. I gasped and then slowly got to my feet. "Trevor?"

"Hey, Kris," he said as he slowly approached me. He looked exactly as he had the day he left for his shift so many years ago.

He stopped before me, smiling brightly, and I cupped his cheeks. "Trevor! It really is you! I never thought I would see you again."

"Yeah, it's been a long time." He brushed his hand over Garda's head. "Garda has been keeping me company."

"I'm so glad he found you."

"Me too." He tilted his head and said jokingly as he continued, "Your life certainly got more interesting after I died."

I threw my head back and laughed. "I guess you could say that. Who knew it could have been that way?"

He ran his knuckles over my cheek. "I always knew you were special and meant for so much more."

"No, you didn't," I said with a snicker.

"I did," he said excitedly and let his hand fall to his side, where he brushed it over Garda again. "I knew you were bound for so much more. There was something in you that was always trying to burst out. I guess we know what that was now."

"Yeah, I guess so. How do you know about it?"

"I have met a few of your friends."

"Friends?" I glanced around, but all I saw were vast rolling hills with green fields and a small lake to my side. "What friends?"

He looked over his shoulder, and I followed his direction but saw nothing. "I wish I had time to tell you more." He closed the distance between us. "Your life is not done, Kris. You need to go back. You have much to accomplish and people who need you very much."

"What? No! I want to stay here. I want to talk more."

He held my face. "I wish you could, but it's not time. I love you, Kris. I will always love you." He leaned forward, and the moment his lips touched mine, the light began to diminish, and I felt myself being sucked back into the darkness.

I fought it at first. I didn't want to leave Trevor or Garda—I hadn't had time to say goodbye to either of them. I wanted to know who had told Trevor things about my life. A few seconds later, I felt the burning inside my veins again and gasped as a sharp burst of energy shot through my chest.

My eyes opened, and I saw faces around me, but one second later, I succumbed to the darkness again, and this time there was no bright light to meet me.

I DON'T KNOW how long I remained in the darkness, but it seemed like forever. My body had been on fire, but now it only simmered with pain and heat. I knew that people had fed me. I recalled the taste of several different types of blood dripping down my throat, but I could not decipher it or enjoy it. I was in some odd limbo.

My mind shut down for a while, and I welcomed the rest. When I felt myself waking again, the world around me was getting lighter, and I hoped to end up back where I had been. Perhaps Trevor would tell me who his friends were.

Only this time, as I blinked my eyes, I was standing at the top of my hotel in Philadelphia. The lights of the city spread out around me. I glanced back and found a young woman standing there.

"Who are you?" I asked cautiously.

She slowly walked closer to me, and I took in her long red hair and clear blue eyes, knowing, without knowing, who this young woman was. "Hello, Mom."

"Briella?"

She grinned. "I thought it might be better to speak to you as a woman rather than a child."

"How are you doing this?"

"I'm special."

I chuckled. "Yes, I know that, but how can you do all of this? You can communicate with people, see the future, and visit me—" I glanced around, unsure of where I was even though I recognized it. "Where are we?"

"Inside your mind."

"You came to see me inside my mind?"

"Yes, we have much to talk about."

"What?" I put my hand up. "Wait! Before we talk about other stuff, am I dead?"

"You died, but they brought you back."

"Am I going to survive?"

"That's up to you, but before you decide, there is something you will need to do."

"What is that?"

"You are going to have to kill Joseph Portage."

I stared at her, then laughed. "How will I kill anyone when I'm living between life and death?"

"There is a way, but you will have to find it. Only after he dies will our breed live in peace for many years. If you do not kill him, he will continue ruining everything, and more of our breed will die. I have seen it both ways. I have seen our breed prosper with his death and our existence vanish because he remained alive."

"Okay, but how am I supposed to do that?"

She shook her head slowly. "I don't know—at least not yet. I only know you have to do it while you are here."

I frowned. How was it possible to kill anyone when I was barely alive myself?

She hugged me tightly. "I love you, Mom. I know you will figure it out. I have to go. Don't give up. I will revisit you soon. You need to rest."

She let me go and spun, running toward the edge of the building and jumping off. I gasped and rushed to the ledge, but before I could reach it, the lights faded around me, and I was left floating in the darkness again. This time, I dwelled on everything that she had said.

CHAPTER TWELVE

HUGH

One minute I am helping obtain detailed information. The next, I heard a bloodcurdling scream from Kristin as if she were being ripped to shreds. Every inch of my body was on alert as I shoved people to the sides. Seconds later, I saw her lying lifeless on the ground, Zander over her, begging her to wake up, and then a sweet, soft voice drifted into my head.

"Hello, Father. I look forward to meeting you, but first, you must help Mom live. All of you must use your reborn power to bring her back. Do it now and bring her home as soon as possible. It's the only way she will survive." The voice was gone a second later. Perhaps I should have questioned it, but I didn't. What did we have to lose if we tried? I jumped into motion, telling everyone to put their hands on Kristin immediately.

The scene before me was chilling as Angelina struggled to heal her sister and bring her back. I had never seen Lena control so much power, but would it work?

Since I met Kris, I have considered her larger than life—as if nothing could stop her. She was always so strong—physically and mentally—and so full of life. Now she was dead—or nearly, and she was pale and limp. Her bright-red hair was such a contrast to her porcelain skin.

I was probably not the only one amazed that what Angelina did for her worked. There were several gasps as Kristin's chest came off the floor and she sucked in a breath before dropping back to the expensive carpet that covered the room.

Zander carried Kristin in his arms, and I moved right in front of him, unceremoniously moving the people in our way out of it. With Kristin going down, the people in the building were animated and moving around quickly. Some asked others what they saw, and others rushed toward the room we had just left as if prepared to fight. Guns were drawn, and there were aggressive words to protect the president.

For a moment, I wondered if the others we left behind would be all right, but I was only worried about getting Zander and Kristin out of there. Corbin was right behind us with Angelina, several guards, and a few human-turned joined us before the truck was on the road.

The human-turned immediately began to shield the truck from anyone trying to locate where we had all gone, and we raced through Washington streets to escape.

I was amped up for a long time, but eventually, I sank to the truck's floor and began to dwell over everything. I couldn't believe that Kristin had died. I also couldn't believe that my daughter had spoken to me mentally. She was merely an infant, so how did she even know how to do that? It didn't make sense, but Briella was different from the other children.

Were there any limits to what she could do? Even when she was in Kristin's belly, she had communicated with Isaac and knew I was in trouble. She had spoken to me from hours away and told me what needed to be done. She hadn't just shown me images but spoken words way above her ability. How was it possible?

I stared at Kristin's profile and tried to speak into her mind. *"Please wake up, Kris. I need your help with our daughter. She needs you."* I glanced around at everyone who was either staring at Kristin or had their eyes closed. *"We all need you."*

I hoped for some sort of reply, but there was nothing. Only silence, and I took a moment to focus hard on Kristin. Her mind was utterly void of anything. It was like a dark wasteland, and I shuddered as I retreated into myself. I had never seen a blank mind before, and knowing nothing was going on in her head made me wonder if her brain worked after that high-voltage electrocution.

I kept those thoughts to myself as we continued to drive to the compound. As we approached the mountain entrance, I looked forward to getting there. I was finally going to be able to see my daughter face-to-face and touch her.

The moment I saw the woman holding Briella, my heart began to beat faster, and I moved immediately to her, taking my tiny daughter into my arms as a joy I had never felt began to spread through me.

"You are so tiny. How can you possibly be able to communicate with me? Did I imagine it?"

Briella cooed, and her bright-blue eyes were clear and happy as she looked up at me and reached for my face. I heard her voice again. *"Father, finally, we meet. I have looked forward to being with you. Thank you for bringing my mother home."*

I spoke back into her mind. *"She will survive?"*

"I do not know. She has a journey she must take, and then she will have to decide if she wants to come back to us."

I stared at her. *"She has to decide to come back?"*

"Take me to her. I need to speak with her."

"Briella, she's not there."

"She is. She is in another place, and I can get there, but I need to touch her."

I brought her into the other room and laid her beside her mother. We all left the room, and as I went, I realized I was afraid of what she said—not only about how Kristin had to decide to come back but because my tiny infant of a daughter could travel to where Kristin's mind was.

"Are you alright?" Angelina asked as we left the apartment.

"Yeah." I glanced at Corbin. "It's just bizarre to have full conversations with Briella when she is only a few months old."

"I can't even imagine what that is like," Angelina said. She looked down the hallway. "Well, lead the way. It's not like I know my way around here."

I led Corbin and Lena up the stairs to the command floor. They were taking it all in as we went to the conference room, where I knew they would all be waiting.

Scarlett stood as we entered. "How is Kristin?"

"She's alive, but barely," Lena said.

"She is going to need time to heal," I added.

"But she's going to live?" Scarlett asked.

"Yes," Angelina said immediately, although I wasn't sure. After what my daughter said, I was conflicted.

"Well, will someone please explain what the hell happened out there, and who is this man with you?" Hazel asked as she sat beside Scarlett and eyed Corbin up carefully.

"This is Corbin," Angelina said. "He is Alex's son also and mated to Hugh and me. Henry raised him."

A few murmurs shifted around the room, and Ben Tremblay spoke up first. "A triple mating? Is that possible?"

"Yes, a triple mating is possible, and we all share each other's abilities, although only slightly. Mostly we have enhanced our own abilities quite a bit."

Ben studied me. "And you are all right with sharing? You didn't strike me as the kind of man who would share what he coveted, Hugh."

"Yes, I am fine with this arrangement." I glanced at Corbin. "The three of us are good together, but our relationship is not of concern here. We need to discuss what we are going to do about Portage."

"Is he the one who attacked the mistress?" a man who worked with Ben Tremblay asked.

"Yes, he is." The three of us sat, and between us, we recounted the story of what happened. As we finished our conversation, Rane popped his head into the room.

"Cameron is on line two for you guys."

Scarlett leaned forward and put the call on speaker. "Cameron, you have quite a few of us here in the conference room."

"How is Kristin?" he asked immediately.

"She is stable for now," Corbin replied as I lowered my eyes. Was she?

"Clayton and Henry are here with me. We are glad to hear you all made it safely there. We sent people to search for Portage, but he vanished."

"Do we have any idea how he accomplished this? Kristin had the building frozen."

"Yeah, the people who attacked her entered the property after Kristin released the compulsion. They weren't bothered by it in the slightest. We found them on security. They walked right in, met with him, and he directed them where to go. Then he vanished." He paused as we all absorbed his words. "It appears they were all under *his* compulsion because they moved like robots. They never spoke, never looked at anyone. Just walked in and started firing at her as if in a trance."

"I'm not surprised," Angelina snarled. "We never should have trusted that son of a bitch!"

"Honestly, without his people, we might not have accomplished what we needed at the other sites. He did give us a larger headcount," Cameron stated.

"What has happened at those other sites?" I asked him.

"Minimal body count on both sides. Out west, there was a bit more bloodshed on our side."

I heard a short gasp and turned to look at Paxton. Gideon was out west.

"Have you heard from Gid?" Corbin asked as he looked at Paxton.

"Yeah, Gid's okay. Minor injury. He's already healing." I heard a whoosh of air come from Paxton, and Garrett rubbed her arm.

"That's good. I'm glad he is okay. What's going on there?" I asked.

"Well, the president is making a formal announcement here soon. I wanted to reach you guys so you could watch it. The order has already gone out to cease and desist all action against the breed. It will take a while for it to all die down, but we are discussing what repercussions we might have if we defend ourselves now."

"Good. Is there anything that we can do here?" Ben asked.

"Just get Kristin back on her feet. Kincaid is pretty upset about what happened to her. He had no idea that Portage had that planned, although I figured out that Portage somehow compelled him to get Kristin alone."

"Portage compelled the president?" Corbin asked.

"Yeah, he did. I'm not sure how, but he did," Cameron said with a sigh. "Get ready to turn the news on. The president is just about to speak. We will be there with him as ambassadors to the breed. That's what he named us. He wants to work together to fix this and allow us to live harmoniously."

"And you believe him?" Hazel asked.

"I do. His words are honest."

"Except," Angelina started, "he's been compelled by Portage."

"Yeah, I was thinking that you, Angelina, might want to meet with him and make sure that all the compulsion is out of his system."

"I can't leave Kristin's side right now," Lena answered, looking flustered.

"I know you can't, but I was thinking of bringing him there."

"What?" several people echoed at once.

"Relax, it's just a thought. We will see how things go in the next couple of days. I have to go. Watch the news." He hung up without another word, and Hazel grabbed a remote control and turned on the virtual monitors around the room.

Angelina reached for my hand and Corbin's, and the three of us sat there, waiting for the president to speak about our future.

CHAPTER THIRTEEN

ANGELINA

I was more tired than I let on. Not only tired but worried. What if Kristin didn't make it? What if I had fried her brain circuits when I manipulated all that energy through her? What if she woke up as a vegetable?

I shuddered slightly, and Hugh and Corbin squeezed my hands tighter to reassure me that everything would be all right. None of us could know, but I had to believe it would be.

The president came on the screen, cleared his throat, and looked straight ahead at the camera. He looked like he had been through the wringer today. Well, welcome to the club. "Today has been a monumental day in American history. We are finding many things that we believed to be true are indeed not." He paused and lifted his chin slightly. "For over half a year, we have been hunting people of the vampire species and brutally murdering them. We did this out of fear and anger. We took a situation that we thought was a vicious attack on our people and turned it into a civil war and a hunting expedition to rid our world of them.

"Since the vampires became known to us a few years ago, there has been a lot of fear and questions about them." He sighed softly. "Unbeknownst to me, members of our government secretly sought out vampires and imprisoned them in an underground facility in Ohio. They were locked up in cells and tortured. They were also experimented on and killed. That is not okay. That will *not* be okay in the future. We do not lock people up for no reason, and we do not torture and kill them. We will no longer do that."

He cleared his throat. "That facility was destroyed, and many humans were killed. There will be consequences for those who were involved in destroying it, along with consequences for those who built and maintained it against my knowledge. We will not play favorites. Both sides are guilty of vicious and dangerous acts."

He glanced to the side. "Today, I had the honor of meeting several people who oversee the vampire breed. They were honest, caring people who shared a vision of us living side by side in a world without all these vicious killings. They have no interest in taking over our world and controlling humans as we might have once thought. If that had been the case, they could have come here and slaughtered everyone, including me. They didn't. They came in peace to talk about a resolution.

"For thousands of years, they have lived around us, mingled in our societies, and worked jobs right at our side. When they became known to us, it struck fear in us, and this was understandable, but instead of trying to learn about them, to befriend them, we labeled them as violent predators who were out to kill us all." He smiled slightly at the screen. "I have seen differently. I met personally with Mistress Kristin Armstrong and Master Zander Armstrong today, along with several members of their governing board. I believe they want peace, and it is time to grant them that."

He turned serious again as he stared into the camera for a moment. "As of now, anyone who detains, tortures, or kills a vampire for unjust reasons will be taken into custody and prosecuted for the crimes. New laws will be enacted to protect them, just as we protect other Americans. This information might raise concerns for many of you, but know that most of the vampire population does not want to war with us. They want to live in peace.

"There is one faction, run by a man named Joseph Portage, that is a rogue group of vampires with a different agenda, and those people will be tracked down and dealt with in a new court that will be overseen by vampires and humans together for just punishments."

He clasped his hands in front of him lightly. "You do not need to fear these people as most of them do not wish us harm. Over the next few months, we will have the opportunity to learn more about them. They will share with us, and we will learn to integrate with them. There will be no more bloodshed between us."

He lowered his eyes for a moment. "To the Mistress and Master, I give you my sincerest apologies for what has happened on our soil. You have my word and the word of the American people that we will do everything we can to form an alliance between our groups to make this nation great again. Good night, and Godspeed."

The camera view changed, and news reporters began speculating about what had happened. We watched for a few seconds, then lowered the volume as we all began to speak over the top of one another.

"Did we really do it?"

"Do you think he will stand by that?"

"What is he talking about, a vampire and human court?"

Hugh put his hands up. "Whoa! Let's take this one day at a time. Of course, we have a lot of work to do, but let's take this as a win."

Hazel sighed. "I have a feeling the humans are going to think we did something to him to get him to say that."

The phone rang on the desk before us, and Scarlett hit the button. "Yes?"

"It's Clayton. Did you all see it?"

"We did," she replied. "Do you believe him?"

"Yes, we do. We spoke for a long time after you guys left. He is determined to make things better. It will probably get worse before it gets better, but we have to make sure the breed knows to be on its best behavior."

"We will have Zander get the word out."

"How is he? How is Kristin?"

Everyone in the room looked at me. "As good as can be expected, Clayton. In fact, I need to go check on them."

No sooner had those words left my mouth than Zander's voice burst into my mind. *"Lena! I need you now!"*

Without a word to anyone, I was out of my seat and flashing to the door. When I stepped out, I couldn't remember what direction to go in, but Hugh grabbed my arm and began to run beside me, leading the way. Behind us was Corbin. I heard a few more feet pounding the hallway but didn't look behind me.

A few seconds later, we reached their apartment, and Isaac had the door open, a blank expression on his features as he watched us speed past him and into the bedroom.

Zander was leaning over Kristin, shaking her as he shouted, "Wake up! Don't do this, Kristin! You can't keep doing this!"

I dropped to my knees beside the bed. "Did her heart stop again?" I asked, but I already knew by the silence before me.

"Yes! Do something!" he shouted.

Corbin stopped me as I began to grab hold of her hand. "No, wait. Let me try something." He put his hand on the center of her chest and closed his eyes as he focused. "Zander, let go of her."

Zander pulled back, and Corbin shocked Kristin. Her body jolted like a rag doll dropped to the ground, but her heart remained still.

"Do it again!" Zander snapped.

Corbin focused one more time and again let loose a shock. This time Kristin's lips parted, and a small burst of air released. We could all hear her heart beating again, and I grabbed her hand after Corbin nodded. I focused on her body, drawing strength from Hugh and Zander as they put their hands back on Kristin and worked on repairing more of the damaged tissue deep in her chest and head.

"Jesus, she's got to wake up. We can't keep doing this to her," Zander muttered as he put her hand to his lips and kissed it. "Wake up, baby. I need you to come back to me."

After I finished, Hugh sighed and sat back on the floor, saying, "Briella told me something earlier."

"What?" I asked.

"She said that Kristin has to do something, and once she has done that, she will decide if she wants to come back or not."

"What the fuck are you talking about?" Zander growled. "Of course, she wants to come back."

"Wait, when did she tell you this?" I asked him.

"When we first got back. Briella said Kris has something to do, and then she must decide."

"And you believe an infant?" Corbin asked skeptically.

"Yeah, I do." Hugh shrugged.

"What the hell can Kristin possibly do in this position? She's barely alive. She can't do anything," I stated.

"I don't know. I'm only repeating what Briella said," Hugh growled back.

I looked at Corbin. "I am as confused as you are about how she can communicate with anyone. Much less that she knows anything about what is going on and how to fix it."

"Zander, you need to feed," Hugh said from beside me, not commenting on what I said.

"I'll feed later."

"No, he's right. You need to feed. We all do. With the energy we expend doing this, we all need to keep our strength up."

"I'll stay with her, and you go feed. Angelina and Corbin can fill you in on what's going on," Hugh told him as he got off the floor and rounded the bed.

"I can't leave her."

"Zander, get your sorry ass off the bed," Hugh growled roughly.

Zander glared at him. "And what if I don't?"

"Then I will drag your ass out of here. I have used the least amount of energy out of all the people here. I can feed her while you recharge."

Zander snarled slightly, and Hugh put his hands up. "Hey, I share her blood too. You do remember I was mated to her for a while, right? Besides, we need your head in the game here. Things are changing, and you are the master."

"Zander, come on," Corbin said quietly. "Let Hugh take over for a few minutes. She's in good hands, and you know it."

He sighed wearily. "Fine." After brushing her hair back from her face, he kissed her brow. "I'll be right back, Kris. Come back to me."

I kissed Hugh on the cheek, took Zander's arm, and walked him from the room. "Isaac," I said as we entered the living room. "Can you have some people brought down for us to feed from? Preferably human blood as it will be stronger for us."

"I will do that." He glanced at the playpen off to the side where Briella had her feet in the air and was pulling at her socks, cooing as any other infant her age would do. "Watch Briella."

"Of course," I replied as he left the room.

Zander retrieved Briella and held her tightly in his arms as he came to the couch and sank to the cushion. He stared into her face as she put her hand on his cheek. He smiled, and his eyes filled with tears. "I will trust you on that."

"Trust her with what?" I asked as I studied the child.

Zander smiled for the first time since Kristin went down. "Come here and meet your niece."

"I'm not into babies."

Zander laughed. "Come here and speak with Briella."

The child watched me, and I rolled my eyes, but I went to the couch and sat down as Zander handed her over.

"Briella, meet your mom's sister, Angelina."

She had incredible blue eyes, and her hair was the same dark shade of red as ours. Briella took one of her chubby hands and put it to my cheek, and a moment later, I heard a soft, sweet voice fill my mind. *"Hello, Aunt Lena. You are as beautiful as my mom."*

I gasped, my eyes shooting to Zander's, and he winked.

"Hello, Briella. How are you able to do this?"

"Because I'm special, I have been born with the memories of both my mother and father. I already know everything about their lives as if I lived them myself. My body isn't ready to do what my mind can do, but I am already older and more intelligent than anyone here."

I stared at her, unsure what to say as she continued. *"My mother has a job to do, and so do you. You must keep her body alive while I guide her to what she must do. Then she can decide if she wants to come back."*

"But what does she have to do?" I stared into her sweet face and saw her features darken slightly.

"She must kill the man who had her killed. Only then will we be safe."

CHAPTER FOURTEEN

KRISTIN

The darkness around me faded again as bright light filtered over me. I didn't fear it this time and lifted my face immediately to the golden glow. The scents were different, with a hint of smoke. A snap and crackle met my ears, and I opened my eyes to find myself sitting in front of the fireplace in the VMF house back in Fawn Hollow. The flames in the fireplace were dancing merrily.

I glanced around, but I seemed to be alone. Beside me was a glass of liquid, and I glanced at the bar to find a bottle of Firefly vodka there. I lifted the glass beside me and sniffed, a smile coming to my lips as the familiar flavors of the Cherry Moonshine filled my nose. I took a sip, savoring it as the fire continued to snap playfully behind the screen.

I stood, carrying my glass with me as I walked around the room. It looked exactly as it had the last time I had been here. Not the time I had come to meet Zander. It had been partially destroyed that day. No, this was how it had been when I lived here many years ago. Above the mantel was my favorite picture, which hung in my office now.

I turned and walked out of the room, heading into the foyer. The room was intact now, and I studied the staircase where the picture had been taken. Rex was just an infant, and all the people I loved were in the photograph. I looked at the door, remembering the day Julian had walked out of it, spewing hateful words.

I turned and looked at the steps again, picturing Zander coming down them as Julian reborn so many years later. My feet led me up the stairs, and I stepped into the room that was once my office. I had done a lot of work in this room. I pictured Trent and Julian sitting in the room while we discussed things.

I left it and returned to the stairs, climbing to the top level where the bedrooms were. I paused by a few doors, remembering people who had stayed in them or lived here during my time in this residence.

I moved on to my room, further down the hallway, and pushed open the door. It looked like I had never left. At the foot of the bed were my old police boots, and on the dresser, all the things I used to put in my pockets. My knife, pens, gloves, and notepad were all there. I set down my drink and flipped through the small spiral notebook, reading a few names I had written there. Some I remembered, some I didn't.

I opened the closet and found all my old clothes there. My uniforms were all neatly pressed and hung in one corner, and I ran my hands over the fabric, noting the smooth texture before I heard something behind me. I spun around and exited the closet, coming up short when I saw Trent lying in the middle of the bed.

"Trent?" I shook my head as I tried to understand why I kept seeing dead people. Trent grinned at me and sat up on the edge of the bed.

"It's good to see you again. I wondered what you would go look at first."

"You've been here the whole time?"

"I have," he commented. "I am always watching you. You were always fascinating, even more so now."

"Why do you say that?"

"Because of all that you are, all that you have accomplished."

"Am I dead now, too?" I asked, still standing near the closet.

Trent stood and approached me. "No, you're not. You're just visiting. It's not your time."

"Then what am I doing here?"

"I felt I needed to explain."

"Explain what?"

He touched my face, the heat of his hand warming my cheek. "Why I did what I did."

"You don't need to. I know that my blood made you crazy."

He laughed briefly. "I wasn't crazy, but it was poisoning me."

"Why didn't you say anything to me?"

"Because I wasn't thinking straight, and I wasn't entirely sure if that was why I was feeling so off. I didn't want to hurt you by telling you something was wrong with your blood."

I frowned. "But you'd hurt me by killing yourself? Do you have any idea what that did to me, Trent? What it has done to Rex?"

His hand dropped to his side. "I know. I'm sorry. I wish I could have been there for both of you."

"Do you? I feel like you took the coward's way out. Maybe we could have done something to reverse the effects if you had said something."

"Like what? Have me mate to someone else? That wasn't going to happen. I loved you, Kristin, with every ounce of my soul. If you had known, you would have forced me to mate with someone else. I could never have left you, but I knew I wasn't right for you. It was with you or nothing. I couldn't imagine living a life without you."

"Trent, you could have fed from someone else. We could have found a way around it without breaking our mating."

He sighed and stepped away, hanging his head. "At the time, I wasn't thinking straight. I told you that." He was quiet for a moment, and I stared at his handsome profile. I had loved Trent very deeply, and it had broken a piece of me when he died.

I approached him, touching his arm. "I'm sorry you didn't think you could talk to me. I miss you very much."

"You mean, you missed me."

I tilted my head to the side. "No, I still miss you."

"But you have Julian now, or whatever his name is."

"Zander. His name is Zander, and yes, I am with him, but that doesn't mean I love or miss you any less."

He twisted quickly, wrapping his arms around me in a smooth movement. He held me tightly for a few seconds, then whispered against my ear, "I miss you too, Kristin. Every day, even here. I'm sorry for hurting you."

I held him tightly. "I miss you too, Trent, and I'm glad we got this opportunity to speak."

He brushed his lips over my forehead, then looked behind him. "I have to go."

"Go where? Why can't you stay with me here? We could fix things. Make things better."

He smiled sadly, running his thumb over my bottom lip. "God, I miss that mouth of yours." He pulled me to him in a rush, kissing me with a pent-up passion that had my head spinning slightly. He pulled back sooner than I wanted him to and stared into my eyes. "I wish we could have fixed things, Kristin, but we couldn't, and now is not the time to discuss them. Someday, we will. You have things you must do first. Use your *dreams*, Kris."

"What?" I asked as he dropped his arms. "Use my dreams? What are you talking about?"

He stepped back like he was being pulled. "I have to go. Use your dreams."

"No! Stay with me! Stay here, Trent. I don't want you to leave." I tried to reach forward to stop him, but I started falling backward, the light fading much quicker than the first time until I was back in the darkness, and my heart burned as if someone had just shocked it.

Trent's words echoed inside me. *Use your dreams*, but use them for what? I felt so confused, and I let myself slide into sleep.

I STILL DID NOT CONTROL my body when I left my dreamless sleep. By the sounds and scents, I knew I was in my bedroom at the compound, not the VMF, and Zander's strong cinnamon scent told me he was beside me. It was like my body was paralyzed as I could not reach him.

Isaac was there also, and I heard him tell Zander to try and sleep. Zander muttered about not being sure he could, but he would try. The room grew quiet, and I listened to the smooth breathing of Zander next to me. His hand held mine, and I wished I could grasp it back as tightly as he was doing mine.

His breathing evened out, and I felt peace fill him, making me feel slightly warm. I focused on him and let myself begin to drift again. If I were supposed to use my dreams, I would have to figure out how to use them. I drifted back into my mind and pictured Zander with me.

After a few moments, I felt him squeeze my hand tighter, his body tensing, and a second later, I was standing back in the president's office. In front of me was Zander. On the other side of the room, I was being lifted off the ground by seven bolts of energy.

Did I remember this, or was he dreaming? Was I in his dream? Zander yelled and threw his hands out. The men flew against the wall, and my body crumpled to the floor in a heap. I winced. No wonder my entire body hurt.

Zander was at my limp side, begging me to wake up, and I walked toward him. I reached out, unsure if I could touch him, but my hand made contact, and he shrugged it off.

"Zander," I called his name, and he spun on his knees, his eyes wide as he stared at me, and then looked at my body on the floor. "Zander, it's okay."

He gawked at me, no words coming to his lips. I took his hand and pulled him to his feet. "I'm right here, Zander. I'm right here."

"Kristin? But you are dead! I saw them kill you. Your body is right here! How are you standing when you were lying there?" He looked at the floor, his blue eyes wide as he spun around in a circle, wondering. "Where the hell did the room go? Where are we?"

"That was a memory, Zander. You were dreaming about what happened. I brought us someplace else. Someplace safe."

"What?" He glanced around again, utterly confused. "If this is a memory, I don't remember it. Have I been here before?"

"You're in a dream, Zander. Remember how you can show anyone anything? I can too. Think back. This is the lake at Eagle Glen. We came here often."

"I'm dreaming this?"

"You were dreaming about what happened, but I stopped the replay. Living it once was enough. I don't think either of us needs to relive it again."

"Are you really here? Or am I making this shit up?"

I chuckled. "I am here, in your dream. Yes, I was attacked, and Portage was behind it, but I'm still here. You all saved me from dying."

"You are barely alive. How are you in my dream?"

"I don't know, but someone told me to use my dreams."

"Who told you that?"

I paused. If I told Zander I had spoken with Trent, would he believe me?

Before I could say anything else, he asked, "Was it Briella? Did she tell you? She said you had something you had to do before you could come back."

"Briella did tell me that I had a mission to accomplish before I could decide to come back, but that's not who told me."

"Then who?"

"Trent."

"Trent?" He looked baffled. "As in Alex's son and your previous mate? He's dead. How could you talk to him?"

I shook my head. "I don't know. He's not the only one I have spoken with, though. I saw Garda and Trevor, the man I was married to as a human."

He looked momentarily concerned. "When did you see them?"

I shrugged a shoulder. "I don't know. I can't tell time here."

"But you saw them both?"

"Yes."

He glanced around, staring out over the water for a few seconds before he spoke again. "Your heart has stopped twice, Kristin."

I studied him, letting those words filter into my mind. "Perhaps I saw them when my heart stopped."

Zander grabbed my face. "Don't you fucking do that again! You got that! Don't you let your heart stop, Kristin! You can't die on me."

"I'll try not to, Zander, but I don't have much control over things here."

"But you have control over this. You're here, so you have more control than you think."

"Perhaps, but tell me what's going on with the president and our people?"

"I don't know everything, but I think he's making changes. He wants the war to end. Clayton, Henry, and Cameron are there working with him, but I don't know much more."

"Why not?"

"Because I haven't left your side. I can't leave you. I'm afraid if I do, you will be gone when I come back."

I stepped closer to him, pressing my lips to his in a quick reassuring kiss. "I'll be here, Zander. Or at least I will try to be here, but you need to lead our people. You must get on top of this and ensure the president follows through."

"I will when you are better."

"No! You need to do it now. You need to show yourself and lead our people. You need to work with the president and solidify things. You are the master, Zander, and it is your responsibility."

He rested his forehead on mine. "But I can't leave you."

"Zander, I'm right here. You have obligations. If you were in my place, would you not want me to do everything I could to ensure our breed has a future?"

"Yes, of course." He paused, looking thoughtful. "Why can't you come back to me in real life?"

"I have things to figure out."

"Like how you can kill Portage?"

"Yes, like how I can kill Portage."

"Maybe you can do this to him. Kill him in his dreams."

"I'd have to find him. I'm not sure I know how to do that. I figured this out because you were beside me, and Trent told me to use my dreams."

"He really told you that?"

"He did."

"What else did he say?"

I relayed my conversation with him and Trevor and then leaned forward and kissed Zander again. Zander cupped my cheek when we finished, his blue eyes shining brightly with unshed tears. "Please do not leave me again. I could not bear for you to die, Kristin. I just found you again."

"I will try not to, Zander, but you must lead our people. You have to let them believe I am healing and will be all right."

"You will be all right."

I smiled at him, trying to ease his worries, but I wasn't sure if I would. "I love you, Zander."

"I love you, too."

"You need to rest a little longer and then get to work."

"I don't want to leave you."

"You must. Our people need you."

"Fine, but wake up soon, please. I need you."

"I love you," I told him again and kissed his lips softly. "Now rest."

I felt him wake up a few minutes later. He sat straight up in bed, grabbed my hand, and kissed it. "I sure as hell hope that was real, Kristin. Don't go anywhere. I need to get upstairs and see what is going on. You stay here and get better. I love you." He kissed my still lips, and then he rushed into the bathroom.

A moment after he left, a tear slipped from my eye and ran down my temple into my hair. If only waking up was as easy as dream walking was.

CHAPTER FIFTEEN

ZANDER

I showered and changed clothes, then paused by her side again. Had my dream been real? Could she visit me in my dreams? It was a lot like my ability, so why not.

"I am going up to the office. Don't you go anywhere," I said quickly and kissed her once more before I rushed from the room and up the stairs. I was just topping them when I ran into Corbin.

"Hey, is Kris okay?" he asked quickly, looking alarmed to see me.

"Yeah, she is." I smiled at him, finally feeling like everything would be okay. "I have some work to do. Would you be able to sit with her? Your gift comes in handy if her heart stops again."

"Yeah, sure. I'll go down there now."

I slapped his shoulder. "Thanks, brother."

He laughed. "Kind of neat to have a brother."

I started to walk away, walking backward as I spoke. "Yes, it is. Hey, where is Angelina?"

"In Kristin's office with Hugh, Ben, and Scarlett."

"Perfect," I replied and headed down the hallway. When I stepped in, Angelina burst from her seat.

"What are you doing here? Is Kristin okay?"

"She's the same but told me to get to work."

"Wait! She's awake?" she asked hopefully.

I shook my head and chuckled. "No."

"Then how did she tell you to get to work?" Hugh asked.

"Because my beautiful mate can dream walk, that's how."

"Dream walk? What the hell is that?" Scarlett asked.

"It is similar to what I can do. I can bring people into my mind and show them a place they have never been. She came into my dreams while I was sleeping. At least that's what I think she did."

"How do you know it wasn't just a dream?" Ben asked, seemingly not convinced.

"Because she brought me back to Eagle Glen Lake. I haven't seen that place in a long time and haven't thought much about it."

The four of them looked at each other, and then Lena asked, "What else did she say?"

"She told me to get my ass back to work." I snickered as I came around the desk. She was going to survive. She would return to me, and now I needed to do as she asked—get back to work.

A few people chuckled, and Lena said, "Now, that sounds like my sister."

"Yes, it does. I asked Corbin to sit with her while I am working, so let's not waste time. Fill me in on what is happening and what you all think needs to be done."

Ben grinned as he leaned back in his seat. "It's nice to have the master back at the helm, not that having the mistress there wasn't as nice, but welcome home, Master."

I studied him and thought about his words. A very long time ago, I had deferred the position of master over to Alex. I didn't want the headaches associated with leading and overseeing the breed, but not anymore. I was ready to take over and fulfill my destiny.

"It's nice to be home," I replied to Ben. "So, what do we know? How was the information received from the president?"

Scarlett said, "There have been a few polls that the news agencies have spoken of. People are happy to hear that the president has ended the violence. Some still believe we don't have a place in society, but for the most part, it is positive."

"There will always be those who hate us," Hugh commented.

"Yes, and those who want to be us," Angelina added. "I saw another poll that said twenty-five percent of Americans would become vampires if they could."

Scarlett sighed. "I feared that would happen."

"It was always a possibility," I replied to Scarlett. "Although I didn't expect that high of a percentage."

"I think it is probably higher," Lena stated with a grin. "I think many people are afraid to admit it publicly."

"Well, we are going to have to be careful and not start turning thousands of humans," I told the group. "I don't think the president would like us doing that."

"Perhaps not, but could you see it if, one day, a vampire was president?" Hugh said with a chuckle.

I scoffed. "I don't see that happening anytime soon."

"I don't either, but it's a funny thought," he said.

"Maybe one day we will see that. I'd just be happy if we could go about our lives like everyone else without worrying someone would hurt us around every corner."

"You and me both," Angelina said with a weary sigh. "I'm so tired of hiding in the shadows. After being out there during that mess, I'm ready for fun." She grew quiet for a moment. "Maybe I'll be able to get my club set up now."

"What club?" I asked her.

"Before all this, I was working on a new dance club in the hotel."

"We will have to find out if Kristin still owns the hotel. I don't know if we can access our properties or assets. Or at least Kristin's. I don't own any property besides the beach house."

"Some of them we do," Scarlett jumped in. "I have had people checking on those kinds of things. The hotel was taken over, but we might be able to get it back."

I thought for a few seconds. "Do we still have the VMF house in Fawn Hollow?"

"Yes," she replied.

"Good, then one of the first things I want to do is get people there to repair it. When they captured Kristin and me, I can only assume they did some major damage to the property. I want that restored. There are a lot of good memories there."

"And some bad ones," Lena muttered and then threw a smirk in my direction.

I smirked back at her. "Yes, and some bad ones, but that place means a lot to Kristin, so I want to get it fixed for her. It will be a nice surprise."

"It would be a nice surprise," Lena replied.

I glanced around the room. "Has anyone heard from Clayton, Cameron, or Henry recently?"

"Yes, they are trying to find a way to bring the president here."

"Here? Why?"

"To show him that he can trust us and hold up part of the bargain Kristin offered him," Scarlett stated.

"What did she offer him?" I asked as Scarlett looked at Ben, Lena, and Hugh, and I got the distinct feeling I wouldn't like this. "Out with it," I barked.

Ben leaned forward in his seat on the couch, "Kristin told him that she would give him a tour of the compound and start sharing our history and a list of people in our organization that had abilities."

"Bullshit! She wouldn't do that."

"She *did*, Zander," Scarlett stressed. "Although she told him that she would only share the names of people who had approved it. If people wished to remain quiet about what they can do, we would have to respect that."

"And how many of our people will opt to let them know?"

"Well, the humans are already familiar with quite a few. All those locked up in the facility are on their radar."

"So. Isn't anyone worried that they will do what they previously did and lock everyone up?"

"Kristin implied that if he or others did that, any treaty would be over, and they would see the wrath of Kristin," Lena stated. "I'm pretty sure he's afraid of her. He asked about her earlier today."

I leaned back in the chair and tapped my fingers on the desk. "That's something else Kristin said. She told me we had to tell everyone that she is recovering and will return soon."

Scarlett raised a brow. "Did she happen to mention when she would be back?"

I shook my head. "She is trying to figure out how to do whatever she has to do."

"Kill Portage," Hugh stated gruffly. "Did she mention how she would do that when she's unconscious?"

"Nope, but..." I paused.

"But what?" Angelina jumped in when I didn't continue.

"There is something else you guys should probably know. When Kristin's heart stopped, she saw other people."

"Excuse me?" Lena screwed up her face.

"She saw her old husband, Trevor, the first time it stopped, and Garda, her old dog. The second time her heart stopped, she spoke with Trent."

Everyone was silent for a few moments. Finally, Hugh asked, "You mean she died and went to heaven?"

"I guess." I shrugged.

"That's not creepy or anything. I wonder if Trent was as crazy as he was before he killed himself," Angelina commented with a chuckle.

"She said he was fine and explained why he did what he did."

"I wish he would explain that to his son. Rex hasn't been right in the head since I told him that his father committed suicide."

Scarlett asked in jest, "When has that child ever been right in the head?"

"Maybe when Kristin wakes up, she can tell him what he said," I stated.

"Maybe." Angelina grew thoughtful. "I wonder why she saw her old human husband, not Alex. It seems weird that she would see that guy. They weren't married all that long, and it was years ago."

"Who knows," Hugh replied to her.

"Okay, so what else do we know?"

"Why don't you give Clayton a call and speak with him? Maybe they have some new information," Ben suggested.

"Good idea. Does anyone know his number?"

Angelina got up and dialed the phone, putting it on speaker as it began to ring. Clayton answered a moment later.

"Hey, Clayton. It's Zander."

"Zander, how is Kristin?"

I hesitated just a second, not sure what to say. "She's okay."

"You don't seem so sure of that answer. Has something else happened?"

"Yes and no, but right now, she is doing all right. She hasn't woken up yet, but..." I paused and then laughed. "It's complicated."

"Well, as long as she is doing all right. I'm glad I got a chance to talk to you."

"Yeah, why is that?"

"Because I'm going to bring the president to the compound in a few days for a brief visit."

"Are you sure it is wise? What if this is just a trap to find our stronghold? What's to stop them from blowing up the mountain the minute he is gone?"

"Because they aren't going to know where he is. It's all hush-hush, but we are sneaking him out for a few hours, and then we will bring him back."

"Get the hell out of here. Are you trying to tell me that he will come here without his security detail?"

"He is bringing four, but we will remove their GPS trackers before we get on the road."

"GPS trackers?"

"Yes, all of them are implanted with trackers so they can always be located. I will ensure they are removed, and then we can bring him under the radar. It's going to be tricky, but it will work."

"Okay, if you say so. Anything else we need to know?"

Clayton paused. "I'm also bringing someone else back."

"Who is that?"

"Her name is Michelle Becker. She works for the president."

"Wait a second. Kristin mentioned her name and said we should bring her back, but I completely forgot about it in the chaos. Why exactly is she coming back here?"

"Because she's a reborn."

"How do we know that?" Angelina asked with her brow furrowed.

"After Hugh was turned, we took DNA samples from people. Do you remember when we did that, Lena?"

"Yes, I do."

"Well, those samples confirmed what we needed to know. Humans have forty-eight chromosomes; vampires have an extra one, but reborns have fifty. By testing their blood, there is a way to tell if someone is a reborn."

"That is very interesting, but how do we know she's a reborn?" Scarlett questioned Clayton.

"When we first discussed the raid of the White House, Kris requested detailed reports on every person who worked here. We found an anomaly in Michelle's medical records. We had her blood retested and found it had fifty."

"Why does Kristin want her to come back here?" I asked, and Clayton grew quiet. "Clayton? You there?"

He sighed heavily. "You'll probably not like the answer."

I clenched my jaw and growled, "Out with it, Clay."

"Kristin wanted her brought back for you, Zander."

"For me?"

"In case she didn't make it. Kristin wanted you to have a reborn that you could mate with."

"What the fuck!" I barked. "You have to be joking?"

"No, sorry. I wish I were."

"Yeah, well, that's never going to fucking happen. If Kristin doesn't pull through, I'll wait until she returns, but there is no way I will mate with someone else."

"She was only thinking about what was best for you, Zander," Ben said from the other side of the room. "You might not like the idea, but I understand why she thought so."

"Yeah, well, I'll be sure to have a word with her when she wakes up because the last thing I will do is let her dictate whom I will mate with if she dies."

"Let's just hope she doesn't die," Hugh said softly.

"Yeah, I'm with you there," I replied sourly.

CHAPTER SIXTEEN

CORBIN

The last thirty-eight hours had been a whirlwind—from the attack on the White House to the devastation of Kristin's injury to planning what would happen next. None of us had gotten much rest, as we had been taking turns staying with Kristin. I was bone-tired like everyone else.

Now it was my turn to stay with her. I lay on the bed beside her, wondering if things with the president would go as planned. What were the odds that he would arrive here and the mountain wouldn't be bombed after he left? I know I wasn't the only one worried about that.

I had seen similar concerns in both Angelina's and Hugh's minds. None of us had to speak about them. We all knew what the other ones were thinking.

I settled back against the pillow, closing my eyes. I'd had a much different picture of what we would have done after the initial attack. I had hoped to strengthen my relationship with Angelina and Hugh and enjoy what we had.

Of course, I'd been hoping that Hugh would have been willing to step up his game and allow himself to take what he wanted. I was all for being his bottom and letting him sate his wicked desires as

Angelina looked on, or better yet, let me simultaneously nail her to the mattress.

I began to relax and drift into sleep as I thought about it. I pictured Hugh on his knees, sucking my cock as he stared at me with those fucking sexy blue eyes. Angelina would have her hands running over my back as she looked over my shoulder, loving what she saw.

"I feel like a voyeur," a voice said from near the door of the room I'd been in.

My head snapped toward the door, and I frowned. I glanced over my shoulder, wondering why Angelina wasn't making a wisecrack about her sister being here, but Angelina was gone. So was Hugh. The only thing still in place was my raging hard-on. I snagged a pillow and covered myself.

"What are you doing here?"

She shrugged. "I'm practicing."

"Practicing?"

"Yes." She glanced away and then looked back, taking a moment to study me from head to pillow.

I laughed uneasily. "Are you thinking of doing a triple mating?"

She rolled her eyes. "Thank you, but no. As fun as that might be, I'm quite satisfied with my mate."

"Then if you aren't here to practice that, what are you here to practice?"

"I'm practicing my dream walking."

"Ah, yes. So, I didn't unintentionally bring you into my dream because I harbored some weird fantasy of having sex with you too?"

She laughed. "God, no! At least, I hope you don't think like that."

"You're safe. Your sister is enough for me."

Her smile was tender. "I'm happy to hear that. It is good to see Angelina as happy as she is. You and Hugh are good for her."

"I hope we will be good for her for years to come."

"I am sure you will be." She looked around the room and frowned. "Where are we, by the way?"

I scanned the room. "Um, this was where we lived while you were locked down in the compound."

She stepped away from the door, glancing at the memory of my room. "Hmm," she murmured. "You know I had no choice when I told her to leave, right?"

"I don't know what led up to it. Lena didn't speak about it much. I know she was angry, and I think part of her was really sad, but she survived."

"I knew she would. My sister is resourceful."

"We almost didn't, though." I went to stand and thought better of it, but then I remembered that this was my dream, and I instantly made myself dressed. She peered at me as I stood, noting my clothed body and nodding.

"Thanks for getting dressed."

I chuckled. "You're welcome." She continued to look over the room, and I shifted back and forth on my feet. "Why *did* you send her away?"

She peeled back the curtain that covered the glass walls of the clothing store I used as a room. I wondered what she saw. Could she see the hallway or something else inside my head?

She frowned at the window and let the curtain fall back in place before she went back to looking around the room. "I sent her away because she brought people into the compound that were not allowed."

"Who?"

"Gabriel, Olivia, and..." She paused and pursed her lips. She turned to face me. "And Zander."

I frowned. "You didn't want him there?"

"At the time, I wasn't sure I could trust him."

"You can trust him now, though, right?"

"I trust him with my life, but when she brought him to the compound, I didn't know if I could. All I knew was that Portage brought him up, and I wasn't sure if he was being honest." She shifted her gaze around the room. "He was being honest, though."

"How long did it take you to realize that?"

"Months. I didn't spend much time with him. He accepted his

punishment and remained in his quarters until I decided it was time for him to come out."

"Would you have kept your sister locked up that long?"

She shook her head, her long red hair waving back and forth down her back and peeking around her narrow hips. "No, I wouldn't have. Although I'm glad that I did what I did."

My brows hiked high. "You're glad that you banished your sister?"

"Yes. If I had not, she never would have found you or Gideon. You have both become important to our cause and our family."

"True, but perhaps we could have come together differently."

"I doubt that." She shrugged. "We will never know."

"So, what now?"

"Now, I figure out how to get to Portage and kill him while I'm in this state."

"Do you think it's possible?"

"Who knows, Corbin? I have no idea. Did anyone think that reborns existed? Did anyone think that a reborn would have special powers or that we would be as strong as we are? Did anyone know that having a child with another reborn would create someone as powerful as Briella?"

I shook my head. "No to all of those."

"Then who knows what is possible? All I know is that I need to do what Briella and Trent have told me. I have to find a way to kill him in his dreams."

"Who is Trent?"

"One of my husbands."

I tried to recall any stories about him but couldn't right away.

"He's the one who killed himself because my blood was driving him crazy."

"Ah, okay, I remember hearing that now. Don't you have a son with him?"

"I do. Rex is his son."

"Rex, that's right."

Kristin studied me. "Could I ask you a favor?"

"Sure. What do you need me to do?"

"I need you to watch both Rex and Garrett and figure out which one has been in contact with Portage."

"What? You think one of them has been talking to that guy?"

"Yes, I do, and I'd like you to figure out which one."

"Why me?"

"Why not you, Corbin?" She paused and shook her head slightly. She lifted her face to mine, and I saw something akin to worry in her eyes. "Help me figure out which one of my boys has confided in the enemy." Kristin suddenly looked pale, and she sank to the chair behind her.

"Are you alright?"

"Yes, just tired. Doing this wears me out. I need to go." She inhaled deeply and then opened her eyes again. They were a light silver as she spoke. "Go back to your original dream and pretend I was not here. Please do not tell anyone else what I asked you to do unless you need to."

I nodded and blinked, and when I opened my eyes, she was gone, and I was back on the bed with Hugh sucking my cock and Angelina running her tongue along my neck before she slipped her fangs into my vein. The memory of Kristin being there was like a puff of smoke that vanished as I let myself go with the erotic feelings.

Our bodies moved together, and eventually, I had Angelina on the bed as I moved up her body, tasting every inch I could. I shifted my hips to fill her as Hugh got behind me. I was ready for him to take me as I took her. I was dying to have his cock deep inside of me, and he was lining himself up when I found myself shoved off the bed and blinked to find myself staring at the carpet under a bed, my hard dick inside my pants and throbbing against the floor.

"What the fuck?" I jerked up to see Zander over Kristin, panic in his features. My dream vanished.

"Kristin! Come on! Don't fucking do this again! You have to come back! Goddamn it, Corbin! You fucking fell asleep, and her heart stopped again."

Panic shot down my spine. I ran to the other side of the bed to put

119

my hand on her chest again. Jesus! I had failed her! Oh my god! How long had she been dead?

I shocked her twice before her heart started beating quickly and slowly returning to a normal rhythm. I ran my hands over my head. "Jesus, I'm sorry, Zander. I fell asleep."

"Fuck you, Corbin! We almost lost her! Get the fuck out of here."

I stared at her for a moment. "I'm sorry." I turned and began to walk away, but Zander called out.

"Did she come to you?"

"What?"

"When you were sleeping? Did she visit your dreams?"

I thought about that for a moment, but I didn't remember seeing her. "I don't think so. I don't know. My dreams are fuzzy."

He glared at me. "Get out."

I left, feeling like shit. Here I was, dreaming about getting fucked by my mates while I lay next to the mistress, and her heart stopped. I stood in the hallway outside her apartment and banged my head against the wall for a moment. Jesus, that was so fucking stupid!

I heard voices down the hall, and I turned to look. Two men were coming out of a room, Garrett and Rex. They stopped and looked at me, and Garrett called, "How is Mom?"

I frowned, suddenly feeling suspicious of him. "She's fine. No major changes." I didn't want to say anything to anyone about the fact that her heart kept stopping. As far as anyone knew, besides the elders, reborns, and Isaac, she was recovering.

"Good," he stated, and then Rex and Garrett began to walk away. Something inside me decided I needed to follow them. I quickly headed in their direction, listening to every word they said and not understanding why I would even be interested.

CHAPTER SEVENTEEN

JOSEPH

I wasn't sure how I got out of the White House alive, but I had. My plan had almost worked! I wanted longer to see her suffer before I plunged the stake into her barely beating heart. I had wanted to stare her in the eyes as I had with Alex and inhale the ashes of the great mistress. Fucking Zander! He went ballistic at the sight of her in pain and blasted away as if they were merely ants with just a flick of his hand. Luckily, his mindset went to saving his mate and not hunting me down.

I escaped—but barely.

I jumped into the SUV that Adam had waiting for me. "Is she dead?" he asked.

"I think so," I said with an exasperated sigh. "I'm not sure she could have survived what happened to her, but I didn't get a chance to stake her. Zander showed up too soon."

"You should have let me take him out when I offered," he growled softly.

Maybe he was right, and I should have. Unfortunately, this little piece of me didn't want to kill him—stupid me for caring even the slightest for him. All those years of caring for him, focusing on him, and how he could make my plans work had made me soft.

"Next time," I replied.

"Did Zander see you? Does he know you were behind it?"

"Oh, yes, he saw me, and I do not doubt he will come after me."

"Then we will be waiting, and I will take him out when he comes."

I didn't respond. Perhaps part of me thought I could coerce Zander into my way of thinking. It was a long shot, but maybe all was not lost with him. With Kristin dead, then Zander would take over. I could find a way to compel him back to my side.

I saw Adam glance my way and then laugh. "Don't tell me you still don't want him dead? Seriously, Joe, the kid is not yours, and he needs to be removed from this earth."

I sighed. "I know, but I want to try one last time to see if I can get him back on our side. With the mistress out of the way, he will take control. We could be back in the game if I get him to shift his thoughts."

"I doubt that, and you are pretty fucking stupid to be thinking that way."

I reached over and grabbed his throat. He gagged and tried to shove my hand away, making him swerve on the road. That was the only reason I stopped. I needed to get away as quickly as possible. The last thing we needed was to get in an accident.

"I suggest you remember who is in charge here, Adam."

He rolled his head around on his shoulders, his voice somber as he spoke. "Yes, sir."

We didn't speak again until we pulled into my new hiding location. It was a property I bought years ago in Virginia near Roanoke. It was perched high above the lake, and no one knew about it except Adam.

"I'm going into my study. I want to see what the news is saying."

"Do you want me to join you?"

"No. I want you to start reaching out to our people and find out who made it and who didn't. By now, the fighting should be over. Find out who survived and get them back in hiding."

"Yes, sir," he replied as I stalked off.

I glanced around as I walked. I had only been here one time shortly after I purchased it. It was nice, but I missed my other mountain home. This one was too modern and not earthy enough—too much chrome and marble and not enough wood.

It took me a few minutes to find my study, and when I did, I poured myself a drink and then turned on the television to a news channel. They discussed what had happened and stated that the president would be having a press conference soon.

Good. Hopefully, the pansy-assed president would announce that Ms. Prissy Pants was dead. That was all I wanted. I knew I could get Zander back to my side if she were dead. After everything the humans did to us, I knew I could get him to see the light.

I sat there for hours, watching the reports say the same shit repeatedly. There was an attack on the White House, but the president was alive and safe. There were attacks around the country, and in some places, many people died, both vampires and humans.

Adam joined me a few hours later and gave me a rundown on our losses. Over two hundred were confirmed dead, and about three hundred were still missing. Maybe they went underground or were dead and not accounted for yet.

When the president finally came on, I sat there hissing at the screen as he spoke.

"For over half a year, we have been hunting people of the vampire species and brutally murdering them. We did this out of fear and anger," the president said to the television monitor.

"This president is a fucking pussy!" I continued to listen.

"Today, I had the honor of meeting several people who oversee the vampire breed. They were honest, caring people who shared a vision of us living side by side in a world without all these vicious killings. They have no interest in taking over our world and controlling humans as we might have once thought."

"Yeah, maybe she doesn't, but she isn't around anymore." I laughed softly.

The president continued on the screen. "As of now, anyone who detains, tortures, or kills a vampire for unjust reasons will be taken into custody and prosecuted for the crimes. New laws will be enacted to protect them, just as we protect other Americans. This information might raise concerns for many of you, but know that most of the vampire population does not want to war with us. They want to live in peace."

You have got to be kidding me! She did it! She really fucking stopped the violence. Ha! Just in time for me to swoop in and finish it.

"There is one faction, run by a man named Joseph Portage, that is a rogue group of vampires with a different agenda, and those people will be tracked down and dealt with in a new court that will be overseen by vampires and humans together for just punishments."

My fury rushed through me! "That bitch! That fucking bitch!" I threw my glass at the screen, and luckily it was a virtual one, and the glass went through it and smashed into the wall behind the picture. Shards of glass and liquor flew across the room.

"Maybe it was Zander who got him on his side," Adam said quietly.

I glared at the screen, seething as the president continued. "To the Mistress and Master, I give you my sincerest apologies for what has happened on our soil. You have my word and the word of the American people that we will do everything we can to form an alliance between our groups to make this nation great again. Good night, and Godspeed."

Was she still alive? He made it sound like she was. How was that possible? I saw what the electrical current was doing to her. There is no way anyone could have survived that.

"She's not dead," Adam said in shock. "I thought you said she was."

I burst from my seat, stalking around the room. "There is no way she could have survived." I rubbed my jaw as I walked. "Maybe he doesn't want to announce it right away. They are hiding it."

"Yeah, that makes sense," Adam said softly.

I turned and looked at him. "That has to be it. There is no way she could have lived through that. They just don't want to announce that she is dead yet."

Adam was quiet for a few seconds. "What about what he said about you?"

"What about it?"

"What are you going to do?"

"Nothing! Why should I? No one knows I am here. No one knows about this place besides you and me." I glared at him. "Are you going to give up my location?"

He jumped to his feet. "No! I would never say anything to anyone."

I glared at him, gauging his response. Adam was an ass, but he was a loyal ass. "See that you don't. Leave me. I need to think."

"Do you want me to clean that up?" He pointed at the broken glass.

"No, I want you to get the fuck out of here so I can think," I snapped back.

"Yes, sir." He quickly left the room and closed the door behind him.

I walked to the window and stared into the dark forest. She had to be dead. There is no way she lived through that. I don't care how strong she might be. She could not have lived through that.

But what if she had?

I shuffled back a few steps and sank into a seat, staring sightlessly out the window as I realized something. If Kristin was dead, and I couldn't get Zander back on my side, he would hunt me until he could stake me himself.

If, by chance, she lived, then there was no way I would live much longer. She would stop at nothing to destroy me. A shiver slipped down my spine, and I wondered briefly how many more sunsets I would see.

CHAPTER EIGHTEEN

KRISTIN

As interesting as it was to know that my sister had a three-way mating, I didn't want to stick around to watch them get it on.

Corbin and I spoke for a few minutes, and I began to feel odd. I was suddenly feeling weak, and there was a pain in my chest. I knew I could not compel him due to the mating with Angelina, but I tried anyway. I could only hope that it worked in this state. I had to know who had been giving Portage information, and I knew it had to be one of my boys.

No sooner had I compelled Corbin when I felt myself falling into darkness, and that familiar bright light returned. I wasn't sure if I liked going there, but at least I had been able to get some closure from those I loved. Who would be there next? I sure hoped it wasn't my mother. She was the last person I wanted to see and let's not even talk about Burke, my father.

When I opened my eyes, I was back in the VMF house. The fire snapped in front of me, and another glass of my Firefly Vodka was beside me. I took a moment to sip it and leaned back in the chair. I knew that sooner or later, someone would come to me here.

It didn't take long for a man to materialize in the chair beside me.

His dark hair hit his shoulders, his deep-set emerald-green eyes studying me carefully. I smiled lovingly at him. "Alex."

"Hello, Kristin. It's been a while."

"Nineteen years. Way too long."

"It should be a lot longer." He looked me over. "You look good for someone who keeps dying."

I chuckled. "I would prefer not to keep doing this. Do you have any pointers for me?"

He gave me a crooked smile. "I wish I did."

"I have missed you." I stood and went to him, sitting on his lap to rest my head on his shoulder. "My heart broke when you died."

"I'm sorry. I know it was painful for you when I died."

"It was. It was painful when Julian died, and Trent, but our bond was so deeply ingrained in my soul that I thought my insides were being shredded."

He hugged me tightly and kissed my brow. "I wish that hadn't happened."

"I know."

"You have done very well, Kris. I'm proud of you," he murmured against my head. "You even did things better than I would have."

I chuckled. "Well, I don't know about that."

"You have. I am amazed at your power and the abilities that you have."

"They are something."

"He is good for you."

"Zander?"

I felt his shrug under me. "Or Julian, whichever way you think of him. You two are made for one another."

"I believe that we were. We both had to die and be reborn to get to where we are now. Except—"

"Except?"

"I'm not sure if I will survive. I keep fighting to get better but end up in this place." I sat up and looked Alex in the face. "Part of me wants to stay here, let all the stress go."

"I hope the other part is larger and wants to wake up and return to life."

I sighed. "Maybe. I know Zander will do a good job if I don't."

"But do you want to leave him?"

"I don't *want* to leave him. I want to live a thousand years with him."

"Then it's time to find a way to do that."

"Briella keeps telling me I must find a way to kill Joseph." I pursed my lips. "You know you could have told me he was your brother."

He winced. "I hated thinking that we were related."

"Yeah, well, that would have been good to know. Along with the fact that Corbin and Zander are both your sons."

"You know, I thought about it after Julian died and I found out that his mother was pregnant. I wondered if it could be possible, but you said his heart was staked."

"I lied."

"Yes, you did. It seems fitting that Julian would come back as my son. We were close."

"Yes, you were."

"He will be good at your side."

"If I can make it back. Right now, I can only visit people in their dreams. Briella says I must find a way to get into Portage's dreams, and that's how I can kill him. I just have no idea how to do that."

Alex thought for a second. "I might have an idea."

I grabbed his hand. "Then tell me because I am at a loss."

"You are going to need to use my blood connection."

I screwed up my face. "What? You're dead, Alex, or did you forget?"

"No, I am very aware that I am dead, but three people close to you are not; they all carry my blood. One was very close to your enemy and might have his blood in him. Use that to find him."

"But how can I possibly kill him from a dream? I might be strong, but I can't physically touch anyone or hurt them from here. Can I?"

"I don't know. Did Briella tell you what to do?"

"No, she only told me I had to do it while I was in this state. Do you think I will wake up if I kill him?"

Alex was quiet as he considered my question. "You might wake up, or you might not ever wake up again."

"You think I will die? Like, die for good?"

"I don't want to consider that, but it is possible, Kristin. Not that you won't be welcome here. There are a lot of people who would be happy to have you here."

I sighed and slipped off his lap to look around the room. "I don't want to die, Alex."

He laughed. "Like any of us wanted to die."

"I know," I said as I glanced back at him. "It's just that I finally have Zander in my life, and everything is finally falling into place. I want to be there to see it happen and to watch my daughter grow up."

"She seems rather incredible."

"She is, and I don't want to miss what happens to her."

He stood and came to me, running his hands up and down my arms. "Then let's hope that once you figure out how to kill my brother, you wake up and live for many years to come."

"I hope so." I slipped my arms around him and held him for a moment. "I miss you, Alex."

"I have missed you too, Kristin." He kissed the top of my head. "I am proud of all that you have done."

"I wish you could have been there to help me."

"Yeah, and then Julian would have shown up. I mean Zander."

I pulled back and looked into his face. "It was confusing for a little while."

"I bet. Everything that happens there is confusing, but I try to keep up. We all do. You're a force to be reckoned with, Kristin. Don't give up. I know you will figure out a way to do it." He lifted my chin with two fingers and stared into my eyes. "I have always loved you, and I will love you forever."

"And I you, Alex."

He brought our lips together in a soft, tender kiss, and then he began to pull back as I felt the blackness calling for me. Suddenly, I felt afraid and didn't want to leave him. Alex had always been a comforting source for me. "Alex! I want to stay."

He frowned. "No, it's not your time. The breed needs you, Kris. You have to kill my brother, then you can decide."

I fought the urge to fall. "But what if I let them all down?"

It was getting dark around me, and his image was beginning to blur. "You could never do that. Use your blood, Kristin. Use my blood and yours. You can do it. I know you can."

Those were the last words I heard before I gasped for breath and felt myself settle back into my body, lying in the bed I shared with Zander.

"Jesus Christ, Kris. You gotta stop doing that. You're going to give me a heart attack here. Wake up, baby. Please come back to me."

I wanted to shout that I was there, but my body would not work. I remained still, even as hard as I fought to wake, and as Zander sat beside me, I began to think about what Alex had said.

He had told me to use our blood, but how could I use it? How could I use that against Portage when I didn't know where he was?

I dwelled on that for a while as I listened to Zander speak. He was telling me what was going on, and while I was glad things were going well, I was nervous about the president coming to the compound. Not that I could do anything about it. I was stuck here in this limbo between life and death.

Before Zander left, he fed me, and it was as I was allowing the blood to drift down my throat that I had a thought. Would it be possible to use his blood, and that of Corbin's and Garrett's, to pinpoint where Portage was? Like a locator beacon of sorts?

They shared Alex's blood, and so did his brother. Could I use their blood to find Portage somehow? Was that what Alex was telling me? Use our blood.

If that was how I could find him, how could I use my blood to kill him? I knew my blood was deadly to him, but how could I possibly make him drink from me while I was in this state?

Zander left me, and Isaac came in to stay with me. He laid Briella beside me, and I felt her grasp my hand. A moment later, I was back on the hotel's terrace, and my baby daughter was a grown woman again.

"Hello, Mom."

"Briella, I'm glad you came to see me. I have a question for you."

"What?"

"Is there a way to feed someone while I'm in this dream state?"

"Why do you ask?"

"Because I think I know how I can find Portage and what will kill him, but I don't know how I can do it."

My daughter gave me a smile that looked sinister. Almost as if she were a young Angelina and not my sweet daughter. It caused a shiver to slip down my spine. "If you find him, I can help you with that."

"How?"

"You might not be able to give him your blood in a dream, but that doesn't mean we can't send him a sample. You could compel him to drink it."

"Can I compel someone in this state?"

Briella laughed. "You already did. You compelled Corbin to determine whether it is Rex or Garrett working with Joseph Portage."

I cocked my head. "It worked? I wasn't sure it would work at all being in this state and that he couldn't be compelled because of the mating. I was hoping it would just be a strong suggestion."

"In a dream state, his mind is weaker, and you were able to compel him. You didn't have to, though. I already know which one it is, and don't worry. He won't be in contact with him again."

"Who?"

"One thing at a time. Let's get rid of Joseph first, and then we can fix my uncle."

"Fine, but how can we deliver my blood to Portage if I find him?"

Briella burst forward and hugged me tightly. "You leave that to me, Mom. Find out where he is, and I will do the rest."

"But you are a baby." She spiked a brow. "Physically, you are a baby, Briella."

"I might seem like an infant, but I am far wiser than you and Father put together."

"What does that mean?"

She stepped back. "That just means that one day when you aren't around, I will take over the breed and keep them strong." She kissed my cheek. "I have to go. You have some dream walking to do. Find Portage."

"I need Corbin's and Garrett's blood."

"I'll have them feed you, and then I will return later. Find Portage, and you can finish things."

"What happens after I kill him? Do I come back?"

She stepped back from me. "That depends on you, Mom. You can try to come back, or you can leave us. I'll be fine either way."

She vanished before me, and I frowned as I turned and looked over the city lights I remembered so well. Her words sent another chill down my spine.

CHAPTER NINETEEN

ANGELINA

This compound was a freaking prison. Thank God I had not been locked in here for months. I have no clue how Kristin did it. Or Zander. Jesus, he had spent months in a small apartment. As much as I had hated being out there during the war, I was glad I was there and not here. If my sister survived, I would have to thank her for sending my ass away.

Now I stood on the small balcony outside, wondering what would happen. What if Kristin didn't wake up? What would life be like without my sister? I had never thought about that. Her presence since the day I met her had always been so large.

I had almost lost her once. Shortly after we found one another, and she was pregnant with Rex, she had gone off searching for Julian on the other side of the country. She was captured and barely alive when we located her at our mother's house.

I had never been so afraid to lose someone, and it weighed heavily on my mind. Since then, I have done everything I could to protect my sister. What if it wasn't enough?

What if we couldn't find a way to kill Portage before she died for good? Would we be able to locate him? If he were dead, would we finally have peace?

The door behind me opened, breaking me out of my thoughts, and I glanced back to see Hugh step out. "I had a feeling I would find you here."

I turned to him. "How did you stay locked up here for months? I would have lost my mind."

He chuckled as he came to stand beside me. "It was rough, but I found ways to keep myself busy."

I snorted a laugh. "Yeah, fucking just about any girl you could."

"I could admit I'm not proud of myself for that, but I won't."

"But you won't. I'm not going to apologize for what I did either."

"And there is no reason you should. It all worked out in the end."

"Did it?"

He turned to study me. "We are here and safe. There looks to be peace on the horizon, and we are making plans for the future."

"But what about my sister?"

Hugh turned and took me by the shoulders. "Lena, you have to be positive. If there is anyone who can pull out of this, it's Kristin. The fact that she's alive at all is amazing." He paused. "She wouldn't be if it wasn't for this bonding we have."

I stepped out of his hold. "Probably true, but I feel like I haven't done enough. I should have been able to do more. She's still not out of the woods. Her heart stopped again today."

"Yeah, I heard about it. Corbin was with her when she did, so he was able to get her back pretty quickly."

"What if one time we can't? What if she dies?" I blinked as tears began to fill my eyes. I could not imagine a world without my sister in it.

Hugh wrapped his arms around my waist and rested his chin on my shoulder. "Then don't imagine it, Lena. Kristin will figure out how to do what needs to be done, and then she will return."

"But what if she doesn't?"

He sighed. "Then we will all grieve, and then we will help Zander to get the breed back up to strength, and we will remember all that she did for us."

"She saved me, you know."

"What do you mean?"

"I mean, I almost died once, but she refused to let me. Alex cut a bullet out of my chest on the kitchen counter. We weren't friends then; she could have let me die, but she didn't. Of course, she might have done that more for Olivia and Gabriel because I had sired Olivia, but I think she did it for me too."

"You know she did it for you, Angelina. She loves you. You two weren't close back then, but you are her blood. If there is nothing else I know about Kristin, she protects her blood."

"She does."

The door behind us opened again, and I felt Corbin join us. "There you two are. I've been looking everywhere for you guys."

"I needed some fresh air," I told him as Hugh stepped back, and I shifted to look at Corbin.

Corbin grinned. "I feel you. It's a nice place, but I can't imagine staying in there for months."

"Hopefully, after the president comes here tomorrow, we can try to get back to our lives." Hugh nodded to the forest. "Out there, and we won't have to stay here any longer."

"Let's hope," I agreed. "Anyone else nervous about him coming here?"

"Yes," they replied in unison.

Hugh added, "But if Cameron says he is on the up and up, then we have to trust that."

"You don't think Portage compelled him again, do you?"

"Cameron assured us that the president is being observed, and he's not taking phone calls to protect him of that."

"Well, that's good, but I'm still not sure I trust him. What if this is all some elaborate plan?"

"Angelina, there is no way Portage could have seen this coming," Corbin said, then continued. "Cameron wants you to look into the president's mind to see if there is any compulsion. He already talked to the president, and he agreed it was wise for all our sakes. He doesn't like the idea of someone influencing him to do things. He believes Portage somehow got to him and compelled him to bring Kristin into that room."

"We already know that he can compel over the phone. He did it to me," Hugh growled. "I do not doubt that if he could get to someone like the president, he would."

"Why do you think Portage helped us in the first place?" I asked.

Corbin shrugged as he came to the railing and leaned his elbows on it. "Probably because he didn't think he could win it on his own. He needed our help."

"And we were stupid enough to believe he had changed." I shook my head as I spoke.

"Did we?" Hugh asked. "I mean, did any of us trust him? I know I didn't."

"Yeah, I didn't trust him either," Corbin responded.

"There is no way in hell I would ever trust him," I commented.

"So, none of us trusted him, and with good reason. Hopefully, Kristin will figure out a way to get to him."

"I hope." I turned to study Corbin's face. He looked lost in thought. "What are you thinking about?"

"Nothing," he replied.

"Don't make me break into your thoughts. You know that's not beneath me to do," I said as I punched his shoulder lightly.

He laughed and stood up. "If you broke into my thoughts, you would have seen me thinking about being with my mates."

The temperature in my blood skyrocketed at his words. "Yes, it has been a while since we were together."

"Been a lot going on," Hugh added. The three of us looked at one another, and then Hugh spoke again. "Not much is happening right now. I mean, we could head back to your apartment."

"Work off some stress," Corbin added with a grin as he stepped before me and put his hands on my hips. "I know I could use it."

Hugh shifted behind me, grinding his instant erection against my ass, and my knees grew weak. Thankfully, I had two strong men to hold me up between them. "Why go back to the apartment? I doubt anyone will come looking for us here."

Both men laughed, and Corbin spoke as his face dropped to mine. "Don't have to suggest that twice." His lips took mine hungrily, and I wrapped my arms around his neck as Hugh shifted the hair away from my neck and began to kiss the sensitive skin under my ear.

Corbin had just started to remove my shirt while Hugh was working on my pants when the door opened, and Isaac stepped out. "I'm sorry to interrupt, but the mistress needs Corbin."

All of us froze. Oh my god! Here I was about to have sex, and Kristin's life was hanging in the balance!

Isaac put his hand up. "She's okay, but she needs his blood."

"She's okay? Her heart didn't stop again?" Corbin asked quickly as he stepped toward the door.

"No, it did not. She is fine, but Briella has spoken to her mom and said that Corbin needs to feed her again."

Corbin flashed through the door, and Isaac nodded and apologized again for interrupting before he left Hugh and me alone.

Now I felt frustrated with both sexual need and guilt. Hugh sighed beside me.

"What?"

"I'm still trying to wrap my head around my daughter. I don't understand how she can do what she can do. She's only a few months old. It shouldn't be possible."

"Can you imagine what a child born to Kristin and Zander would be like? Briella told me she has all your memories, and Zander is much older than you. It would be incredible how much knowledge that child might have."

"Let's hope Kristin lives long enough to find out what kind of child that would be."

"Yeah, let's hope." I frowned. "You know, I was looking forward to having sex again. What has it been, two or three days since we had sex?"

"Three, but I think you will live. I promise that when we do, you'll enjoy it."

"Me? What about you? Won't you enjoy it?"

Hugh stared at the trees and then smirked. "Yeah, I'm sure I will enjoy it." He sighed. "But we have to stop talking about it, so my dick can calm down. It's so fucking hard right now I'm not sure I could walk straight."

I grinned at him as I ran my hands over his chest. "I could take care of that for you."

"You could, huh?"

I nodded as I lowered myself to my knees. "No reason we should both be denied."

It didn't take much to get his pants undone and pull his thick erection out. I was on him in a second, and he groaned as I took him deep. One of his hands held the back of my head as he thrust his hips forward, shoving his cock deep into my throat.

After a few minutes, he leaned down and pulled me up before working on the closure of my pants. I helped him by shimmying my hips and getting my pants down to my thighs before he spun me around and pushed me to lean over the railing. He ran his dick back and forth between my legs, pausing at my ass and pressing momentarily before readjusting and filling my pussy.

"You can have my ass if you want it," I told him as he slammed into me.

"Oh, I want your ass," he growled into my ear, "but the next time I take an ass, it will be Corbin's, not yours."

The visual alone took my body immediately over the edge, and I gasped as the orgasm washed over me.

AFTER MY TRYST with Hugh on the outside balcony, we checked on Corbin and my sister. Corbin was coming out of her room when we arrived.

"Sorry, I had to leave," he said.

"Don't worry. We'll make it up to you. How is Kris?" I asked.

"Fine. They wanted me to feed her again, although Zander and Garrett just had. I'm not sure why."

"Who knows," Hugh said. "Whatever works to help her."

"I was going to come find you guys. Isaac wants you to stay with your sister for a little while."

"Me?" I asked, surprised. "Why me?"

"I have no idea, but he said it needed to be you."

"Well, alright then. I guess I'll go lie around with my sister for a little while." I left the men and entered my sister's apartment. It wasn't that I didn't want to stay with my sister; I just didn't want to stay while she was in this condition. It freaked me out a little bit.

Isaac smiled when I entered. "That was fast."

"Yeah, we were already here."

"Well, lie down by your sister and take a nap."

"Why?" I asked him suspiciously.

"Because she needs to speak to you and can only do that while you sleep."

He brushed past me and closed the door behind him as I looked between the door and my sister. She looked to be sleeping, although paler than usual.

I kicked off my shoes and walked around to the other side of the bed. After I climbed onto the bed, I stared at her profile, whispering, "Don't die on me, Kristin. I need you."

I half expected her to laugh, but she didn't. She remained the same, breathing shallowly and lying lifeless. I closed my eyes and willed myself to drift off.

It didn't take long before I was slipping away and found myself standing in a wind vortex very similar to what Olivia had created all those years ago, right after I had turned her. I glanced around the space and watched Kristin step through the wind currents, her hair blowing wildly around her as she did.

"It's about time you came to visit me," she said with a smile.

"You could just wake up and have coffee with me like you used to do."

She looked slightly sad as she replied, "I wish I could. I need your help, Angelina."

"With what?"

"I have a plan, and I need your assistance."

"Anything. What do you need?"

"I know how to kill Portage, but I need you to help me."

A wicked grin began to slip over my face. "You had me at kill Portage. What's the plan?"

CHAPTER TWENTY

HUGH

I was so fucking horny. Even after having sex with Angelina, I was still lit like a live wire. I was surprised my dick wasn't trying to punch through my pants.

I didn't say anything about it, though. Corbin and I went up to the floor where food was served. I wasn't all that hungry, but neither of us had anything else to do.

As we ate, Corbin seemed distracted. He'd glance over to Garrett or Rex, who were both eating at different tables with other people.

"What's bothering you?" I asked him.

"Nothing. Why?"

"Because you seem preoccupied," I replied.

He studied me for a moment and then spoke into my head. *"What do you know about Rex and Garrett?"*

"Um, they are both Kristin's sons."

He rolled his eyes. *"I fucking know that!"*

"Why are you asking? You don't like them or something?"

He shrugged and glanced toward Rex again. *"I don't know. For some reason, I feel like something is going on with one of them that I need to know about."*

"Like what?"

He spoke loudly, giving me a droll look. "I just told you I didn't know."

"Then I don't know what to tell you. They seem fine to me."

He frowned and stared at his plate for a minute. *"Do you think either of them could be working with Portage?"*

I stared at him, then wiped my mouth with my napkin as I leaned forward to lower my voice. "What the fuck makes you say that?"

"I fucking told you I don't know, but I need to find that out. It's weird."

I studied him. *"Has someone compelled you?"*

"No, not that I know of, and that's not possible anyway."

"Have you ever been compelled?"

He shrugged. *"Not recently that I know of."*

"Well, what you are describing—that feeling—that's what being compelled feels like. It's like you have this incredible urge to do it, but most times, you don't even remember wanting to do it."

"Then maybe I haven't been compelled if I know I need to do it."

"Or maybe you have, and it isn't as strong as it should be." I glanced around the room, wondering how I could figure this out. I could take Corbin to Angelina and have her see if he has a compulsion hidden in his mind—or I could try it myself.

My dick instantly got rock hard again, and Corbin raised a brow as if he felt the surge of hormones.

He laughed. "What, getting off once wasn't enough for you?"

"No, never." I grinned. "I have an idea. Finish your food, and then I will try something."

"What?"

I spoke privately to him. *"Angelina can find a buried compulsion in someone's head. Maybe I can find it if I look."*

"Then go ahead and look around. It's not like you can't get into my head."

"I have to be deeper into your head and taking your blood at the same time. I don't think here is the place."

"Ah." He nodded with a knowing smile. *"Probably not, but I bet most people wouldn't mind watching."*

"Shut up." I threw my napkin at him. "Finish eating."

He did, and we went to Angelina's apartment a few minutes later. When we arrived, he pulled his shirt over his head and tossed it to the side.

"Why did you do that?" I asked him, suddenly nervous about being here with him alone.

"Because you need to drink from my vein, and I don't want blood on my shirt. It's not like I have a lot of clothes here."

"Oh," I replied, feeling stupid. He probably just wanted me to dig inside his head and figure out if something was there. I had no idea why I thought it would lead to more.

Okay, so that was a lie. I was hoping he would want more. I hadn't been lying to Angelina earlier when I said I wanted to take his ass. I was ready to take that step, but maybe he didn't want me to.

He paused by the couch and walked past it into the bedroom. I followed more slowly, trying to remember how Angelina had done it to me. She had taken my blood and dug through my mind.

He kicked off his shoes in the bedroom and then sat on the bed. He raised an eyebrow my way. "You coming?"

Not yet, I almost said. "Yeah, how do you want to do this?"

He gave me a slow, simmering smile and lay back on the bed. "With you on top."

"Jesus, man, I need your blood, not your dick."

"But you can have that too," he said wickedly.

I rolled my eyes but kicked my shoes off and then yanked my shirt off and tossed it to the floor. I walked to the side of the bed, and he sat up, putting his hands on my hips and looking up at me. I had the insane urge to kiss him but held myself in place.

He let me go and scooted back on the bed. I crawled beside him, then thought better of it and straddled him. I closed my eyes as I felt his erection between my legs.

"You aren't the only one hard," he stated with another smirk.

"Yes, I feel that."

He ran his palm over my groin, making my eyes nearly roll back into my skull. I grabbed his hand and pulled it away, then took hold of his other wrist and fell forward so that his hands were above his head and our faces were close.

"I need to focus on what I am doing."

"Fine." He seemed disappointed as he turned his face away to bare his neck to me. My fangs slid down, throbbing to taste his blood on my tongue.

I leaned forward, brushed my nose along his neck, and whispered to him, "This might hurt."

Before he could say another word, I latched onto his throat, and his body tensed under me. I sucked deeply, connecting myself with his mind and starting to look around. Memories from many years filtered through my mind, but I forced myself not to dig too deeply and instead looked more on the surface for more recent memories.

He lifted his hips, grinding himself against me as he moaned. I fought to stay on task and finally found a shaded spot that wasn't easy to see. I reached into the area and saw a hazy picture of Kristin. They were standing in a room that looked like an apartment that had seen better days.

"Help me figure out which one of my boys has confided with the enemy." Kristin's voice filled my mind. *"Yes, just tired. Doing this wears me out. I need to go. Go back to your original dream, and pretend I was not here. Remember only what I asked of you, and do not tell anyone else about it unless you need to."*

Her face vanished, and I pulled at the shadow around it to bring it down. I heard Corbin gasp as the memory returned to him, and then I pulled my fangs from his neck and licked at the puncture wounds.

"She compelled me from a dream," he said in wonder.

"I told you she was pretty fucking amazing." I stared down at him and then released his hands and sat up.

"She's not the only one," he said right before he rose and flipped me to the bed, where he lay over me. "That's pretty cool that you can do that too."

"I bet you can too."

"Yeah, maybe," he said as he stared down at me. Neither of us moved, and then Corbin leaned closer and brought his lips to within a centimeter of mine. "I'm going to fuck you now, Hugh."

My body shivered with anticipation, but he didn't give me a chance to reply as his lips crashed against mine. My arms instinctively wrapped around him as he deepened the kiss.

He ground his dick against mine, then shifted and began to undo my pants. I shoved his hands away and worked on undoing my belt and zipper as he rolled to his back and began to undress quickly. I finished before him, and just after he pushed his pants down, I shoved him down and bent over his cock.

"But you got it wrong, Corby."

"What did I get wrong?"

"It's me who is going to fuck you."

His entire body quivered at my words, and his eyes closed. "Please."

I sucked him deep into my mouth, wondering how I could be so excited to have sex with another man. I didn't care; I was just glad he wanted me as much as I wanted him.

He gripped my dick and stroked it for a moment before talking me into doing a sixty-nine with him. We spent a few minutes working each other almost to the ledge, but then he pushed me off and got on his knees, turning his ass toward me and looking at me with so much intensity that I almost lost it all over the bed.

I got behind him and momentarily thought that I didn't have any lube, but one glance at my cock and I saw how slick it was from his mouth, and I knew it would be enough.

I lined myself up with his ass and pressed forward without a second thought. He groaned, and I threw my head back on my shoulders at the tight, hot feeling surrounding me. "Fuck!"

"Deeper," he growled. "Go deeper."

I shifted my hips slowly forward until I couldn't go any further and then pulled back, pushing into him again slowly.

"Jesus, fuck!" I hissed as I pulled back again.

"Again," he said.

I wasn't going to deny him. I thrust faster forward, pulled back almost out, and thrust again as he whimpered slightly. One of his hands had moved down between his legs, and I knew he was stroking himself.

I kept on for a few more thrusts, feeling the urge to come climbing quickly.

"Yes! Fuck, yes!" he called out as I thrust harder and kept going. I started to come, and he jerked under me as his orgasm began.

Once we stopped moving, we collapsed to the bed, and I rolled away from him, trying to get control of my breathing.

It was only then that we noticed Angelina standing in the doorway, a sly grin on her lips. "Well, well, well. That was almost as exciting to watch as it would be to participate in."

Corbin chuckled.

"You guys just couldn't wait, could you?" she said as she came to the bed.

"I guess not," I replied.

"Good. I'm glad you got that out of your system because we have some business to attend to."

"Wait, before we do that"—I leaned on my elbow—"I need to tell you that Kristin compelled Corbin while she was in a dream."

"Yes, I know."

"What?"

"She just told me about that."

"She did?"

"Well, she wanted me to check to see if it worked, but you could figure it out on your own."

"I was able to dig it out as you did to me."

"Good."

"How did she, though? I thought people couldn't compel us," I asked.

"I have no clue. She shouldn't have been able to. Perhaps because he was sleeping, she was able to do it."

"We will have to figure that out later," Corbin stated. "What else did Kris say?"

"I will tell you guys later. Get showered and dressed and meet me upstairs. I need to go speak with Zander."

"You're not going to tell us anything she said?"

She started toward the door. "If I stay in here any longer, none of us will be going anywhere for a while. As much as I'd like to do that, this takes priority."

"What is the priority?"

She grinned, her eyes sparkling wildly. "To kill Portage."

She was gone before we could say anything else, and then Corbin stood and held his hand out to me. After he pulled me up, he said, "I'd offer to wash your back, but I think that would only delay us further."

I chuckled. "Yeah, I might have to agree with you on that."

CHAPTER TWENTY-ONE

ZANDER

Isaac had told me that Garrett and Corbin needed to feed Kristin.

"But I just fed her," I replied.

"Yes, but she needs their blood too."

"How do you know this?"

Isaac glanced at the infant in his arms, and I held up my hand. "Never mind. Briella told you. Got it."

"Has she been wrong, sir?"

"Well, I am hoping she is wrong about Kristin having to decide if she wants to come back or not. I think Kristin wants nothing more than to return to us."

"I believe she does, Master."

"Isaac, please call me Zander when it's just us."

"Sir, you are my master, just as she"—he gazed adoringly toward Kristin—"is my mistress. You both deserve respect."

I touched his arm. "And we know that, but you are more to us than just a servant or protector, Isaac. You are a friend and family to us. You don't see Angelina calling me master, do you?"

He chuckled. "She's not one for propriety, sir."

I laughed softly. "No, she's not, but please know that I am speaking for Kristin and myself when I say you are more than just someone who works for us."

His eyes dropped. "I thank you for that, sir."

"Zander."

He lifted his face to me. "Zander."

I slapped him fondly on the arm. "Why don't you get Garrett to come down and feed Kristin, and then we will locate Corbin."

He handed Briella to me. "Of course, si—Zander."

I snickered as he did an about-face and hustled from the room. After he was gone, I sank to the couch with Kristin's daughter in my arms. "Are you and your mom cooking something up?"

Briella cooed, stretched, and touched my face. *"We have a plan, and Mom needs the blood of all who are close to Alex to do it."*

"The blood of Alex? Why does she need that?"

"To locate his brother while he sleeps."

Well, that made sense. "What happens when Kristin finds him?"

"Then she can kill him."

I shook my head. "Briella, can Kristin kill someone in a dream?"

Briella wiggled slightly. *"Anything is possible."* She removed her hand, closed her eyes, and promptly fell asleep.

Anything is possible. Well, that was very true. God knows that we have seen a lot in recent years, from the human-turned being able to control elements to dead people being reborn into someone new. I studied her little features, wondering what she would be capable of when she grew up.

No doubt she would continue to amaze people. As I laid her down in her bassinet, I again wondered what a child between Kristin and myself would be like. Would our child be as gifted as this one was?

I was still dwelling on that when Garrett returned with Isaac. "Is Mom alright?"

"There has been no change."

"Isaac said you needed my blood." I glanced at Isaac and saw him shake his head ever so slightly.

"Yes, we do. Maybe having your blood would help your mother get stronger."

"Sure, I'd be happy to do what I can."

"I appreciate that, Garrett."

Garrett and I went into the bedroom, where Kristin remained unconscious. It was the first time Garrett had seen her in days, and he gasped. "I thought she was getting better."

I studied him. "We wanted people to believe that she is. We can't have people thinking that she might not pull through."

He stared at her for a long moment. "Is she going to die?"

Technically, she had died several times, but I didn't want to get into the details. "I hope not, Garrett. I need her—we need her."

He nodded slowly. "Yes, we do." He turned to me. "Not that I don't think you couldn't handle controlling the breed, but she does have more experience."

I smiled at him to tell him I was not offended by his comment. "She has more experience, and I hope she can help me adjust better in time." I paused, thinking. "But if she doesn't make it, I will need your help. I know that your mother trusts you a lot, Garrett. She says that you will be the one to succeed her one day."

"She does say that, but I know I am not ready." He shifted toward me. "But I can help you with whatever you need."

I put my hand on his shoulder. "Let's hope I don't need your guidance for a long time. Why don't you sit on the bed by the pillows and feed your mother for a few minutes?"

"Sure."

I watched as he got situated and leaned back against the wall as he began talking about the injuries that had finally been reported. "We lost about eighty people from here. Better than most places."

"But still not great. The loss of eighty of the breed is still not good."

"Do you think so? I think that losing eighty is better than losing a hundred."

"It is, but losing one life is too many."

"I guess."

I smiled at him. "That is part of being a good leader. It is a difficult thing to ask our people to go to war. The decision to do such a thing is never taken lightly because we know there will be casualties."

"Yeah, I get it."

"The sad part is that people assume others will die and do not prepare themselves for the loss they might have to deal with."

He looked at Kristin. "Are you prepared to lose her?"

The thought of losing Kristin was like a knife to the gut. Already I had lost my mating bond with her, but that could be repaired as long as she lived. "I will never be prepared to lose her to death, but if that happens, I will learn to accept it."

"Can you accept it?"

"I wouldn't have a choice, Garrett. Yes, I love your mother, but I also love our breed, and I can't just crawl into bed and wish my life away. I have too many other people to worry about, too many people looking to me for comfort and advice on how to proceed."

"Why did Mom not kill everyone at the White House when she attacked?"

I paused as I thought over his words. Did he believe that his mother hadn't been right to do that?

"What would you have done differently?"

I shrugged. "I don't know. I might have been more inclined to take out all those I could as I went in."

"What would that have proved?"

"That we are the stronger species."

"Are we?"

He scoffed. "Of course we are."

"Physically, we are, but they have a lot of great minds that can make them stronger than us. It's not just about brute strength, Garrett. They have the numbers to defeat us—the proof of that can be seen in the events of this last year—even if they don't have the physical strength. Your mother wanted to show them we didn't want to hurt them. That we could coexist and work with them. If we worked side by side, we could accomplish more."

"Do you honestly think that we can work with humans?"

As I studied Garrett, I felt my hackles begin to rise slightly. I pushed off the wall and went closer to the bed. "Garrett, I think the question is, do you think we can work with humans?"

He stared at me for a moment, then looked at his mother. His wrist was over her mouth, and some of the blood ran down the side of her face. He leaned over and wiped it off, then held his wrist up. "Do you think that is enough?"

"Yeah, that should be good." I approached him and took his wrist, licking the slice he had made to feed his mother. "Thank you."

"No problem." He hopped off the bed.

"You didn't answer the question," I said as he began to walk out.

"Because I'm not sure of my answer."

I frowned slightly. "Why not?"

"Look, I get that we aren't supposed to think of ourselves as the superior race, but look at Mom, at you. Aren't you guys superior to everyone else?"

"No. Not at all. We can die, just like everyone else, Garrett." I pointed at his mother as I spoke. "We can get gravely wounded too."

He laughed. "Everything can die, but you guys are superior. All of you reborns are superior to the rest of us. It makes me wonder if I should even rule one day. Why would people listen to me after having the great Kristin and Zander presiding over them."

"We might have evolved, but that doesn't make us superior, Garrett."

"I think it does. What is going to happen now? I mean, now that we know how to find reborns. Is she going to start searching for them, get them to breed more children like Briella? Are you guys going to have children? I might not have a front-row seat to what that kid can do, but I have heard some things, and it's impressive as shit."

"It is impressive, but I don't know that we plan to build our breed of reborn children. I think it is more important others rebuild our breed."

"I think we would be better off if people like you did. Then we would be the better species." He glanced at the door. "I have to go. I'll talk to you later, Zander."

Before I could reply, he was out the door, and I frowned again. The conversation that we had shared left me nervous. I remember Kristin saying she thought one of her boys had been in contact with Portage. Sadly, I had a feeling she might be right.

Had Garrett been hiding his true feelings all this time? Had he been working with Portage behind our backs? Did he even know he was working with the guy?

I sighed, went to Kristin's side, and took her hand in mine. "I need you to wake up. Too much is happening here, and I need your help." There was no response, and I kissed her hand before I left her alone in the bedroom.

ISAAC WAS WITH HER NOW, and I was in Kristin's office. Angelina, Corbin, Scarlett, and Hugh were with me.

"What did she say to you when you visited her?" I asked Angelina.

"She said that she knows how to get to Portage. She is using the blood from Alex to link to his scoundrel brother."

"That's why she wanted to feed from Garrett too?"

"Yes, you and Corbin share Alex's blood, but Garrett's blood is the freshest, so she wanted some of his. If she can tap into Alex in that blood, she might be able to locate Portage."

"But how is she going to kill him in a dream? Is she going to suggest that he do it and make him commit suicide?"

"No, she's going to use her blood," Angelina replied.

Hugh chuckled, and Corbin looked confused. "I know she compelled me in my dream, but I don't think she can physically touch someone. How is she going to get him to drink from her?"

"Well, that is where I come in," Angelina said with a smile.

"Go on," I encouraged her.

"Once Kristin knows where he is, she will tell me, and I will go to him. I'll compel someone where he is to give him her blood."

"How the hell is that going to work? Is she going to be able to talk to you from that distance?"

"No." She shook her head. "Zander will stay here and dream walk with her to find the location. Once she gives it to him, he will relay the information to me."

"And you think you can walk right up to his front door and knock?" Scarlett asked.

"I don't think he would answer for you," Corbin replied.

There was no way I would let Angelina go to that man. "No, I'll go. You stay here and dream walk with your sister."

"No, she told me to do it."

I glared at her. "If you think for one second that I am going to sit back while you hunt down that bastard and kill him, you have another thing coming. After everything that son of a bitch did to me and what he did to Kristin to put her in this state, there is no way I won't be the one to deal the final blow."

"She wanted you here," Angelina said with pursed lips.

"Yeah, well, that's not happening. I will be the one to take the man down."

"Like he'd open the door for you any more than he would for me," Angelina muttered.

"No, he won't open it for me either, but I am damn sure Adam will be with him. He doesn't go anywhere without that whack job."

"Zander, Kristin said she wanted you to stay with her here."

"And I already told you no." I stood and scanned the room. "I watched him kill my real father. I watched him kill Kristin. For years, I stood around waiting for him to use me as a fucking pawn. If anyone gets to kill him, it's me."

Corbin shifted in his seat. "Not to annoy you, Lena, but I think Zander is right. Of all of us here, he deserves to be the one to stake the man."

Lena stared at Corbin momentarily, then shifted her eyes to Hugh.

"I agree with them," Hugh finally said.

"I am not staying here while you kill him. I am going with you."

"I'll stay here with Kristin and dream walk with her," Hugh offered. "Then I can communicate with Lena immediately after I wake and tell you guys where to go."

"Corbin stays too, in case Kristin needs help," I stated.

"I can do that," Corbin replied.

I nodded. "Sounds like a plan. That sound alright with you, Lena?"

"Fine, but I want to be the one to take Adam down."

"That's fair, although he is the one who killed me all those years ago."

"I will not go on a field trip with you and not kill someone." She pouted.

I chuckled. "You can kill Adam, Lena. I'll let you have that one, but Portage is mine."

I sat down, skimming my eyes over the group as I thought about the pleasure of running a stake deep into his black fucking heart.

CHAPTER TWENTY-TWO

KRISTIN

The part of the conversation with Briella that stuck with me was when she said, you can try to come back or leave us. She would be fine either way.

It bothered me more than I wanted it to.

What did she mean, I could try to come back? Did she think that I couldn't? Or that I wouldn't be able to? Did she even want me to?

She was an infant and might have my memories, but did she understand them?

I wished she would return and speak to me again, but she didn't. I didn't know whether she thought I had everything that I needed or because she didn't want me to return after this was over.

I wanted nothing more than to finish the task that I needed to do, but I didn't have shit in terms of knowledge of how to complete it. So far, I had cryptic clues: dream, Alex's blood, and my blood. I understood I needed to use their dream state to visit, but how would I use my blood to kill Portage? I couldn't physically be there, so unless I sent someone to him who carried my blood, I wouldn't be able to kill him that way.

Briella said she could help with that, but I would need to find him first. I had already enlisted my sister to help me with this. Perhaps she could carry my blood and give it to him once I located him. That was the closest thing I could come up with regarding a solution.

I focused on the blood coursing through my body. Like when I removed my blood from Joshua's body, I located and focused on the particles traveling through my veins that belonged to Alex. Once I figured out how to do it, it was easy to recognize them.

I used those particles to build a homing beacon and let myself drift, searching for similar blood. The problem was that I was inside the compound, and the only people I found were Zander, Corbin, Garrett, and a few others, like Rex, with traces of his blood from generations removed.

If I were feeling one hundred percent, maybe I could have gotten outside the compound, but my body was still struggling to recover. Even with the blood pouring down my throat from so many people, I knew my body was not healing correctly.

Was my body failing me? Had Portage gotten what he wanted after all and destroyed me? Would I ever be able to recover?

I heard a sound near me, and I focused on the air passing through my nose to catch an evergreen scent. Gabriel had come to see me.

"Hey, sweet potato." He spoke as he ran a finger over my cheek. "I think you have slept long enough. Maybe you should wake up and stop being a couch potato."

I wasn't sure if I wanted to laugh at the nicknames he gave me or cry because I wanted so badly to wake up but couldn't. I was becoming claustrophobic in my own body.

The bed dipped beside me, and he took hold of my hand. "They say that if I lie down beside you and fall asleep, you might visit me in my dreams." He grew quiet. "I bet you need a friend about now, huh? Why don't we try it? I'm going to take a little nap, and you visit me. Okay?"

I felt him lie down, and he squeezed my hand tighter as he pulled it closer. "I need to know you are alright in there, Kristin. Come talk to me."

Gabe settled beside me, but it took a while before he drifted off. Shortly after he did, I found my way to his dreams.

He was sitting on a bench, his face directed at the ocean before him. I glanced around but didn't recognize the location. I waited a few moments to see what he would do, but he just remained there, watching the waves come in and out.

I approached him, and he turned when he heard my footsteps. "Took you long enough."

"I was waiting to see what you were dreaming about."

He grinned as he stood, approaching me and making me feel small with his tall frame. "I was sitting here waiting for you to come. I thought you might like this place." He held his hand out to the ocean.

"I do. Where is this?"

"North Carolina. This is where I was living before all of this." He pointed at the bench. "That is where I spoke to Zander and brought up your name to see if it would jog any memories."

I nodded. "I'm glad that you did."

"I'm glad it worked, and I'm glad that it worked out for all of us." He took my hand and pulled me to the bench. "Let's sit and chat."

"What do you want to chat about?" I asked after I'd taken a seat and leaned back to stare over the ocean. It was the first time I realized the sun was up, and it wasn't nighttime in his dream. "You dream about being at the beach during the day?" I chuckled.

"Yeah, I do. Ironically, I was here at this beach when I met Sabrina in a bar while on vacation with some friends." He grew quiet momentarily. "I like to come here to remember what it was like before it all happened."

"Before you were a vampire?"

He nodded. "You ever do that?"

I stared at the water, watching the waves break close to shore. "I used to, but not recently. I have too much to deal with every day. I don't get much time to walk down memory lane."

"Then maybe we should do that. What do you miss most about being human?"

I laughed. "Being human? Huh, okay, the obvious." I pointed at the sky. "I miss the sun."

He smirked. "I do too. What else?"

"Um." I thought for a moment. "I miss being oblivious."

"Oblivious?"

I nodded. "Yeah, oblivious to what was happening in the world that I couldn't understand or explain. Even as a cop, I saw things that never quite made sense, but when Dawn died at the lake, and you and Julian showed up, the blinders were removed. A part of me misses how simple life was as a human." I laughed. "I remember always feeling stressed about what needed to be done and rushing to get through life, but once I turned, I stopped with that stress and took on a whole different one."

"Well, you didn't really take that on until Alex died."

"Oh, no, that's not true. Do you know what it was like finding out I was a reborn vampire and no one understood what that meant? Then Alex was kidnapped, I met Trent, Angelina appeared, and I killed Burke. All of that was stressful on a whole new level."

"Yeah, I guess so, and Olivia being kidnapped and then killed probably didn't help any."

"No. God, do you remember the look on Mick's face when he saw Olivia dead? Talk about stress. I wasn't sure what to do about him or what to tell him."

"That was when we learned you could compel without taking blood."

"Yeah, it was. It was stressful to keep the secret about what we were."

"Has it gotten easier since the world knows we are here?"

"No, not really. I used to think that it might be, but then I realized there was a reason we kept it so quiet—to protect the humans and ourselves from all this happening."

"Well, you helped to find a solution, and the president will be here soon to finish talking about it."

I sighed. "Not with me. He will speak with Zander."

"You could wake up and join the conversation."

"I'm trying, Gabe. I just can't figure out how to get to Portage in a dream state."

"You didn't have any trouble getting to me."

"No, because you are right here. I can't get outside the walls of the compound. No matter how hard I try."

He looked thoughtful for a moment. "Then leave the compound."

I laughed. "I can't just get up and walk out of here."

"No, but someone could take you out. Have Zander take you someplace else."

"No, Angelina already told me that Zander was going with her. He pretty much demanded to be the one to stake him. I have to give them a general location so they can be ready. Besides, I have no clue where I could go."

Gabe grew thoughtful for a moment, then turned to me. "Do you trust me?"

"Yes, you know I do."

"Then let me take you someplace."

I thought about that. "We would have to keep it quiet from Zander and Angelina, but Hugh and Corbin would have to know."

"Why?"

"Because Corbin is the one who brings me back when my heart stops, and Hugh is supposed to dream walk with me and relay the location to Angelina."

"We would have to bring Josh too so he can hide you from others."

"That's true. That would be a good idea."

"What is Zander going to say about this?"

"Nothing."

He frowned. "Nothing? Somehow, I think he will have a lot to say about this."

"He's going to say nothing because he will not know about it—Angelina, either. We won't even be able to tell the others until right before we do it. We will have to wait until they are gone, and then you can move me."

"That sounds like a plan."

I grinned at him. "Yes, it does."

"Now, how about we come up with a plan on how to wake you up?"

I laughed. "One thing at a time, Gabe. One thing at a time."

CHAPTER TWENTY-THREE

CORBIN

The plan was decided—at least as much as we could plan. Hugh and I would stay at the compound with Kristin. Hugh would dream walk with her, help her locate Portage, and get the information to Lena as quickly as possible. I was to keep her alive and bring her back if her heart stopped again during the process.

Zander and Angelina would head out and move around a bit, looking for information until Kristin could give them the exact location.

Everyone else was preparing for the president to arrive, although we had delayed it a couple of days. The elders were all behind closed doors discussing what should be addressed and how much we should allow him to know.

The fact that the president was coming here was huge, especially since no one on his side would know about it. Only four of his most trusted bodyguards would be allowed to join him. The president had convinced Cameron, Henry, and Clayton that he was on the up and up about his visit and didn't have an ulterior motive. He wanted to learn more about us on his own, so he could help make decisions that would be the best for both the vampires and humans.

In the past, he had relied on information given to him, but he told

Clayton that this relationship with us was too important and fragile to leave to anyone else. He no longer wanted plausible deniability concerning our breed.

I respected that. I had always thought he was a good president until all hell broke loose, and he didn't stop it. Now he was stepping up to the plate, and he would help us devise a plan to get the world to calm down. They needed to know we were not threats to them—at least not all of us.

Of course, Portage was still a threat and a risk to all of us—human and vampire. Had he kept his mouth shut a few years ago and not let the secret out of the bag, we would still be living as if we were not different.

But he had opened his big fucking mouth, and I wished I could watch Kristin, Angelina, and Zander shut it forever. Not that Kristin would physically be there.

I glanced around the commons room, where groups discussed the latest news reports. Hugh stepped in with Abina and Violet. Abina was Angelina's daughter, and they seemed to be trying to cheer up Violet, who was Novah's daughter. I hadn't known Novah, but Angelina said she had been sketchy and after power. She had made a play for both Rex and Garrett. Unfortunately, Novah died during the battle.

Hugh put his hand on Violet's shoulder and spoke softly to her, then hugged her tightly and came to join me. As he walked my way, he let his gaze drift over me as if ready to devour me right here.

After he had broken the compulsion that Kristin put on me in a dream, he had taken me in a way we both wanted. There was a different connection between us now, and I knew our relationship with Angelina was cemented even deeper.

"Have you said goodbye to Angelina yet?" Hugh asked as he joined me.

"No, she's with Zander and her sister right now. I was waiting until after she said goodbye to her."

"You think it will work?"

"All we can do is hope it will work."

"What if Kristin can't find him?"

I eyed Hugh. "Are you saying you don't think she can?"

"No. I am sure Kris can, but what if it takes a long time?"

I shrugged. "Then we wait."

"But then Lena and Zander will be out there waiting. Despite what the president is doing, it's still unsafe out there."

"Hugh, Angelina will be fine. She survived months on her own with no one. She is stronger now than ever, and Zander was already strong. Have a little faith in her."

"I do have faith in her. I just don't want to lose her."

"Neither do I." Just then, Angelina came into the commons room.

We both stood as she approached. "It's time for us to go."

I nodded to her, and we followed her out of the room and down the stairs into the garage. Zander was throwing a bag into the back of an SUV.

Gabe and Olivia were with him, and so were Garrett, Rex, and Isaac.

"We ready to go?" Zander asked as we reached them.

"Yep, as ready as we can be." She turned to me. "Take care of my sister and keep her alive."

I pulled her tightly against me. "I promise I will do everything within my power to keep her alive. You focus on yourself. We will be fine."

I kissed her once, and she nodded and turned to Hugh. "Same goes with you."

He chuckled. "I swear, we will be with her the entire time." He hugged her too, and then the two stared at one another. He nodded, and she glanced at me and smiled.

Without another word, she walked away, and I felt her anxiety as if it were my own. Zander was talking to Gabe and Isaac and then said goodbye to Rex and Garrett before he approached us.

"I am leaving her in your hands."

"And we will protect her," Hugh said.

"If you don't, I will stake you myself."

Garrett and Rex walked away, and Zander watched them go. "Keep an eye on them. One might reach out to Portage and tell him what is happening."

I glanced back and watched them disappear up the stairs. "We will keep an eye on them."

"If they do, we won't have the upper hand."

"Do they know Kristin will dream walk to find him?"

He shook his head. "No, we told them that we were searching for him on some credible information."

"Okay, at least they can't tell him about that."

Zander nodded to us and then climbed into the driver's seat, saying before he closed the door, "Protect her as if she were your own."

"We will," I assured him, and then they were gone.

We watched the transport leave the garage, and Gabe joined us. "Why don't we go back to Kristin's apartment and talk about a few things."

"Sure," Hugh said, and we started heading up the stairs. I didn't think much of Isaac as he stayed behind.

Inside Kristin's apartment, Hugh checked on Kristin, and Gabe handed out a few drinks. I sank onto the couch, taking a long sip of the whiskey Gabe had given me. Hugh joined us a few moments later, and Gabe handed him one too.

Hugh didn't sip his; he guzzled it and then set his glass down and sat beside me. "She's fine right now."

"Is there something you wanted to talk to us about?" I asked Gabe, who looked slightly nervous.

"No, not really," he said, and Olivia chuckled.

"Gabe is being shy." She carried the whiskey bottle to Hugh, poured him another glass, and filled mine slightly higher. Then she returned the bottle to the counter and collected two more drinks for her and Gabe. "He wants to toast to killing that son of a bitch."

"I can toast to that," Hugh said.

Olivia held her glass out to us, and Gabe joined us around the coffee table, where we each tapped our glasses together.

"Bottoms up!" she called, and I threw back my drink, leaving the glass empty.

When I set it down, I noticed that Hugh had also emptied his, and Olivia was smiling as she watched him put it down. It was then that I started to feel something deep inside of me. I stared at my glass and then at Hugh. He was blinking and shaking his head slightly.

"What did you do?" I said as I stared between Olivia and Gabe.

The door opened, and Isaac and Josh walked in. Isaac nodded at Gabe while Josh looked at us curiously.

"Nothing that didn't need to be done. Relax," Gabe said, and I tried to fight it, but my mind was spinning.

"You put something in our drinks?" I slurred as Hugh slumped to the side.

"We will explain later," Olivia said. "I promise you; it's what Kristin wanted."

I couldn't speak after that, and I started to slip under as I heard Isaac say, "I'll get the mistress ready to go."

Go? Go where? Where the fuck were they taking her? The last conscious thought I had before my mind went blank was, Zander is going to fucking kill us.

My head pounded when I came to, and I burst into a sitting position and shook my head, trying to get the drugged cobwebs out of my head. Beside me on the bed was Hugh, still passed out.

I climbed off the bed, looking around and not recognizing the place. Once upon a time, it had probably been a very nice room, but now it had spiderwebs in the corners and a thick layer of dust over the old furniture.

Where the fuck were we? Were Olivia and Gabe working for Portage? Had they kidnapped us and brought us to him? Where the hell was Kristin?

I went around the bed and shook Hugh's shoulder. "Wake up!" I hissed at him. He shifted but didn't come awake.

"Damn it, Hugh. Wake the fuck up!" I growled at him, pulled up my power, and sent a light shock into his body.

He jerked up on the bed. "What the fuck!" he shouted. "Why the hell did you just shock me?"

"Because we were drugged and brought someplace."

He put his hand to his head. "Jesus, that's why my head feels like it is going to split in two. Where are we?" He glanced around as he threw his legs over the side of the bed.

"I don't know. Does this look familiar to you?"

He glanced around more. "No, not really. The last thing I remember was toasting with Gabe and Olivia."

"Yeah, they drugged us. The last thing I remember was hearing Isaac say something about getting Kristin ready."

His blurred eyes cleared instantly. "Where is she?"

I shook my head. "I don't know. I just woke up. I wanted you awake before I went looking for her."

"Then what are we waiting for?" Hugh started heading toward the door, but it opened before he could reach it.

"Oh, good, you guys are awake," Olivia said happily.

Hugh had her by the throat instantly. "Where the fuck is Kristin?"

CHAPTER TWENTY-FOUR

HUGH

Gabe was there before I could finish the sentence and touched my arm. Suddenly, the anger that I felt began to dissipate.

"Put her down, Hugh! Kris is fine. She's in her room resting. I'll take you there as soon as I explain."

"What the hell is going on?" Corbin asked as he pulled me back to his side.

"Sorry about drugging you, but Kristin said it was the only way to get you here without a fight."

"Where are we?" Corbin asked.

"At the VMF house," Olivia answered.

"Why the fuck did you bring her here?" I snapped, my anger surging again. "We can't protect her here."

"We can. Kris is safe. Josh is with her, and he's protecting her location. Jett and Ryker are outside her room."

"Why did you bring us here?" Corbin asked again.

Gabe spoke. "Because Kristin needed to be out of the compound to reach Portage. She couldn't get out of the protected walls in her dream state. We decided to bring her here. No one would look for her here, and with us, she will be safe."

"Why didn't you just tell us that? Why did you have to drug us?" I growled toward them.

"Because we feared you would contact her sister, and Zander would learn about it. We need them to stay focused and not worry about her," Gabe replied.

Olivia stepped closer. "Please do not contact her. We need you guys to remain calm so she doesn't pick up on anything. Otherwise, they will return, and we have to finish this."

"This was Kristin's idea?" I asked.

They both nodded, and Gabe explained, "I visited with Kristin, and she told me she couldn't get out of the compound's walls. I suggested we take her out. She thought that was a good idea but feared you two would fight it."

"Jesus, who else knows about this?"

"No one else. Just those who are here."

"You realize they will go fucking nuts when they hear she is not there."

"We know that, but hopefully we can get this done before they even figure out we are gone."

"Where is she?" Corbin asked, stepping forward. "I need to see her and make sure she is alright."

"Come this way," Olivia said and left the room.

"Zander will stake you both if something happens to her."

"Yes, we recognize that threat," Gabe muttered.

We followed Olivia into a long hallway. There was a grand staircase to the right and then a row of doors off to the left. Jett and Ryker stood outside a door at the end of the hallway. Jett grinned, but Ryker looked nervous as we approached.

"You guys better hope she survives this," I snarled toward them.

"Was Isaac in on this?" Corbin asked Gabe.

"Yes, he helped ready the van and carried you down."

I walked past Jett and Ryker and through the partially open door. This room was better taken care of, and the bed was neatly made, with Kristin lying in the center, looking stronger than she had.

Perhaps being here was good for her. Sitting beside her holding her hand was Josh.

"See, she's fine," Olivia said as she dropped to the side of the bed and bounced slightly.

"You're lucky," I replied.

"Now, who will lie down and dream with her?" Olivia asked.

"Hugh is," Corbin replied. "I will keep an eye on her and make sure she doesn't crash again."

"Well, you better climb on because the clock is ticking." She tapped her wrist as if to make a point.

Hugh looked around the room. "Is everyone going to sit here and watch?"

"No," Corbin said. "They were all just leaving."

Gabe touched my arm. "You haven't let Angelina know we are here, have you?"

"No." I glanced at Kristin. "If she said this is how it needs to be, then I'll keep quiet, but if I get in there and she tells me differently, I will tell everyone where we are."

"That is fair," Gabe replied. "We will be downstairs if you need us, but Josh will stay."

Olivia leaned over the bed. "It's showtime!" She kissed Kristin's cheek noisily and then practically skipped out of the room. Gabe closed the door behind him, and then it was just the three of us.

"Do you think Kris really wanted this?" Corbin asked.

"Yeah, probably," I replied.

"Well, then, let's get the show on the road." Corbin pulled a chair over to the side of the bed and got seated while I kicked off my shoes and climbed on the bed.

"Are you going to stay there, Josh?" I asked him as I got beside her.

"Yes, I need to keep hold of her hand to continue hiding her presence. Not that we expect anyone to come looking for her, but you never know who could be traveling in this area. Even in this state, her presence is strong."

I nodded, accepting his answer. "Alright, Kris, let's see if this works." I lay down, and thanks to the residual drugs in my system, I drifted off rather quickly.

When I slipped into a dream state, my room changed and quickly morphed into the club where we had gone dancing one night. Kristin was dancing in the middle of the floor by herself. With a glance around, I realized no one else was there except Josh, and he stood quietly off to the side, watching Kristin's every move.

She turned toward me, smiling. "You came."

I laughed as I stepped onto the dance floor. "It wasn't like you gave me any choice." I looked around again. "Why here?"

She shrugged. "I don't know. I just wanted to have a little fun before we started."

"Have you been able to locate him?"

"Not yet. I have been saving my strength."

"Well, as much as I'd love to watch you dance, you need to get to work."

She sighed, and the happiness on her face receded. "Fine."

Kristin stood in the middle of the floor, closing her eyes and letting her hands float to her sides. "Come to my side and touch me so you can see what I see."

I went to stand behind her and put my hands on her hips to stay out of her way. The moment I did, I felt myself spiral into her mind.

Flashes of random memories and pictures began to fill my head, and I closed my eyes to focus on them. A lake, a woman dead, the scent of leather, of death filled my senses—an old car, Julian and Gabriel inside. The scents of cinnamon and evergreen collided inside my mind as I saw their faces. A parking lot, Julian leaning forward to kiss her, a man's deep voice, Alex staring at her.

She focused on Alex, and the images moved even faster—so fast that I couldn't grasp them, but one thing I could hold on to was the scent of rich coffee and aromatic spices. They filled my mind and grew stronger as I saw her feed from Alex.

There were more memories of Alex and her constantly feeding from him, and then the images changed to Zander, Garrett, and

Corbin. Zander's strong cinnamon scent, Corbin's deep nutmeg scent, and Garrett's light coffee scent filled my head.

All rich spices blended with what I believed Alex would have smelled like. The images slowed and then stopped as Kristin stood in a vortex of wind. All around us, the air was moving as if we were in a tornado. Her head was thrown back, her breathing steady, and the wind vanished, and we could see around us.

The first time it did, I frowned. Before us was a man a bit older than me watching television. As he turned his head in our direction, the vortex shielded us, and we were floating again.

I was confused, but I kept silent to avoid interrupting her. A few seconds later, the air cleared again, and a woman was in a bath. Just as the air currents began again, she spoke. "Who is there?"

We were gone before I could even think to respond. Could they see us? Or were they able to feel us?

We stopped three more times, two more men and another woman, and I was feeling dizzy and ready to call it quits. Kristin had to be tired. Perhaps she needed a break.

"Kris, you should rest, and we can try again later."

"No!" she ground out, and I felt her body shaking slightly. "I have to keep going. I think I found him."

I remained silent, wondering if this was too much for her, but then we landed in another room, and there he was. He was bent over his desk doing something, and he paused and looked around, a frown on his face.

I was afraid to breathe, so I held it, and so did Kristin. He turned away from his desk, looking in our direction. "Adam? Is that you?"

I felt Kristin shaking harder, and then the air was back, and a second later, we were outside the house. "Take a good look," she said. "That way, you can describe it to them. He is in Virginia, near Roanoke, the north side of the lake."

"Okay, that's enough. Let's go! Time for you to go back so I can tell them where he is."

"You go. I will keep watch."

I stepped around her, careful to keep in contact with her. "No, you need to come back. You're worn out. You did what you needed to do."

"I need to finish this, Hugh."

"Not alone, Kristin. Let Angelina and Zander finish this. They have your blood, and they will compel him to drink it and stake him so there is no chance in hell that he will ever return."

She shook her head. "No, your job here is done. Tell my sister where he is. I need to remain here."

"Kristin! You need to come back with me."

She put her hands on my chest. "I need to stay. This is my destiny." Before I could say anything else, she shoved me back, and I flew through the air and crashed into the glass wall of the dance floor. As I slipped to the ground, the club disappeared, and I jerked upright to find myself back in the VMF house.

Corbin's eyes flashed wide. "Did you find him?"

"Jesus Christ! Yes, we found him, and she fucking stayed there. She refused to come back, and he knows someone is there."

I yanked her hand toward me. "Kristin, you need to come back and wake up right now! Do you hear me? Do not stay there!"

CHAPTER TWENTY-FIVE

ANGELINA

The plan was to head toward Kentucky. That was his last known hiding location. As we drove, Zander and I were mostly quiet. Once in a while, we would talk, but most of the time, we remained lost in our thoughts.

Since Kristin had gotten hurt—I refused to look at it as killed—I had dwelled many times about how we had become friends and sisters.

After she had killed Burke, our father, I was torn on how I felt about that. Burke was all I ever knew. He had taught me how to get my way and not to let anything stop me from what I wanted. He was powerful and blunt, and while I knew he'd loved or cared about me, he never came out and said it.

Then he was gone, and I felt slightly adrift, and when I needed help, I had come to Kristin for it. Her world was different, and I learned that early on. None of them were out for power, especially not Alex, the reigning master at the time.

Burke had always said that Alex didn't deserve the position. He made a mockery out of us because he didn't let us live up to our full potential. I had believed what my father had said, that Alex wanted to control our breed. My father only wanted to make a better life for us.

When I came to Kristin for help, I was desperate. I hated that humans were being kidnapped and turned to test theories. Did I think that we should be able to turn humans if we wished? Yes. Did I believe that we should kidnap people to do it? No.

I was shocked when I realized that Kristin's best friend, Olivia, had appeared in Leo's den. I quickly devised a plan to get her out and hopefully get the help of Kristin and her friends to stop what was happening. It had worked.

Olivia got the gift of immortality, and I got the chance to get to know Kristin better. The day I got shot, I never expected to live. I figured I would bleed out and my life would be over, but Alex had saved me, and Kristin had welcomed me into the group.

That was the first time I saw what family was like—how people cared about you and told you they cared. They laughed, cried, and fought sometimes, but mostly they lived happy lives.

From when I came to them until now, life had given me so much more than I could have expected. Yes, the urge for power bubbled to the surface from time to time, but Kristin had always been good about helping me keep it in check. If she wasn't here, who would do that?

I did have mates now, and I knew they would help me, but neither of them would understand me as well as my sister did. Even this last week, as we waited for things to happen, I felt lost in a way that I hadn't felt in over forty years. I needed her back.

While thinking things over, I realized that my father wasn't much different than Portage. If Burke had lived long enough, would he have joined Portage in his fight? I had very little doubt that he would have. Perhaps even I would have been working under the umbrella of Joseph Portage.

The thought made me feel sick, and I hissed under my breath.

"You okay?" Zander asked.

"Yeah, I'm fine. I was just thinking about something, and it turned my stomach."

"What were you thinking about?"

"My father, our father, was very much like Portage. I am pretty sure that if he were alive, he would be helping him. And if he were alive, then I would probably be helping both of them."

Zander chuckled slightly. "Yeah, I can see why that would make you feel sick." He grew quiet. "You've come a long way, Lena."

"Yes, I was thinking about that."

"After you killed Olivia, we all wanted to skin you alive, not your sister. She wanted to try and help you."

"She always saw the best in me, even when I didn't."

"She's good like that."

"She always has been."

He glanced my way. "She's going to make it. I know she will."

"What if she doesn't, Zander? What if she never recovers?"

"She will."

"Zander, we don't know that. I want to think she would, but her body was fried, and when I check on her, it's barely repaired itself, and we have no clue what is going on in her mind."

"Her mind is fine, Angelina. It might be dark and closed off, but we've both seen her in dreams. She is fine there."

"But what if she stays there forever? What if that is the only way her brain will ever work now?"

As he ground his teeth, a muscle ticked in his jaw. "I don't know. Those thoughts have crossed my mind, but I don't dwell on them. I can't dwell on them."

I sighed. "Don't hate me for saying this, but I hope she either wakes up soon or dies for good. Trust me when I say this, I do not want to lose my sister, but I cannot imagine her living like this for years. I don't think it's healthy for us to have her hang on like this."

His shoulders drooped slightly. "I know, Angelina, I know."

"Aren't we supposed to take Route 79?" Zander asked, breaking me out of my thoughts.

I didn't want him to know, but something was going on. I'd been getting odd feelings through my bond with Corbin and Hugh. For a while, they were calm, almost like they were sleeping. I wondered if one of them had slipped into a dream to check on Kristin.

They weren't supposed to do that until we got closer to this region, but perhaps they were checking on things.

"Um, yeah, we take Route 79," I replied to Zander. God knew that I had driven this route enough when I had been looking for intel on the whereabouts of this man.

"Okay. It should be coming up in about thirty miles," he said as I reached deep into myself again to see what my men were doing.

They were quiet, as in really, really quiet, and that wasn't normal. Suddenly, I felt adrenaline course through my body and forced myself not to react. I didn't need Zander freaking out about Kristin.

They were highly excited, and I turned my face to the window, trying to figure out why. *"Hugh? Corbin? You guys alright? What's going on?"*

Neither of them answered me, and the adrenaline slowly subsided. Maybe Kristin's heart had stopped again, and they had to start it. I wondered who Kristin visited with this time.

We were almost to the turnoff when I felt anxiety ripple through me, along with fear and anger. What the hell was going on back at the compound? Had it been attacked?

"Lena!" Hugh's voice exploded in my head. *"He's in Roanoke, Virginia!"*

"Roanoke? Are you sure?"

"Yes!"

Zander was about to make the turnoff. "No! Stay on here! He's in Roanoke!" I grabbed his arm.

"What? Kris found him already? She wasn't supposed to do it yet."

"Well, I'm glad she did. We are only a couple of hours from Roanoke. We would have had farther to go if we had gone that way."

"Why the hell did she search him out now? She was supposed to wait."

"I don't know. Give me a minute. Something is going on," I muttered to Zander and turned inside of myself.

"Hugh, what is going on? Why are you so upset?"

"Jesus, fuck!" he muttered.

"Hugh! What the fuck is going on?"

"What? What is happening?" Zander asked from beside me.

"I don't know. Hold on. Just drive and drive fast," I quickly said to Zander and then refocused. *"Goddamn it, one of you fucking answer me! What is going on?"*

Hugh's anxiety was sky-high, and finally, Corbin was able to respond to me. *"Kristin found him, Lena, but after she did, she literally pushed Hugh out of her dream and stayed there."*

"What? What do you mean she pushed him out of her dream?"

"Just like I said. Kris shoved him out of her dream and stayed there. Hugh will try to fall back asleep, but I'm not sure it will work. He's pretty amped up, and I don't know that he will be able to calm himself down enough to do it."

"Find a way to calm him down! She can't stay there! We are hours from that area, Corbin! She will use too much energy if she tries to stay there while breaking through the compound walls."

"Um, yeah, about that—" He paused. *"We aren't in the compound."*

"What are you talking about?"

"We are at the VMF house in Fawn Hollow."

I gasped. *"What the fuck are you doing there? Holy shit, Corbin! Whose fucking brilliant idea was it to leave the compound with her?"*

"Lena, what the hell is going on? Is Kristin okay?" Zander asked worriedly from beside me.

"Yes," I told him and then growled at Corbin, *"I suggest you get her ass back to the compound before someone finds her."*

"Josh is here protecting her."

"Who else is there, and whose idea was it to do this?"

"It was Kristin's idea, and she planned it all before you guys left. Gabe, Olivia, Jett, Ryker, Hugh, Josh, and I are here with Kristin."

I was fuming mad and trying to remain calm for Zander's sake. *"You better fucking find a way to get back to her!"*

"We are."

"Use Gabe. He can calm him enough to get him back to sleep."

"That's a good idea," Corbin replied. *"In the meantime, he's on the north*

side of the lake. Hugh can send you images of the area once you get closer. Let me try and get him back to sleep."

"You know that Zander will lose his mind, right? You guys are going to get punished for this shit!"

"Look, it wasn't our idea. We were drugged and brought here. This was all the work of Kristin, Olivia, Gabe, and Isaac."

"Isaac! He was in on this?"

"Yes, he was."

I sighed. "Which means that the kid was probably in on it too."

"Probably. I'll be in touch soon."

He was gone before I could reply. I peered at Zander from the corner of my eye. His hand was on the steering wheel, and he was gripping it so hard I thought it might snap. For some reason, he had opted to keep the transport in manual drive, not automatic. He had said something about being in auto the vehicle was easier to follow using GPS.

"So, the good news is that we know where he is."

"What's the bad news, Lena?"

Oh, man, how did I tell him this? At least this idea hadn't come from my mates. "Your mate had an idea, and I'm not sure you will like it."

"What did she do?"

"Well, she had them take her to the VMF house."

"Why the hell would she do that? They can't protect her there!"

"Jett, Ryker, and Josh are there, along with Gabe and Olivia. She's safe—for now."

"What's that supposed to mean?"

"Hugh was in a dream with her, and when they located Portage, she shoved him out." I paused as he glanced at me, his mouth open in surprise. "And she stayed there. She refused to leave, so she shoved Hugh out of the dream after she found Portage."

"Goddamn that woman!" He slammed his hand down on the steering wheel and did the last thing I expected him to do. He started laughing.

CHAPTER TWENTY-FIVE

JOSEPH

I sat on the edge of my seat for several days, waiting for someone to knock at my door—but no one showed. There was little talk of me on the news now. A couple of days ago, they posted a reward for information leading up to my capture, and a few people had said they had seen me here or there, but they were all liars.

No one knew I was here except Adam and the seven other men protecting this house, and they were all compelled to keep their big mouths shut. Now it was a waiting game.

There was also no further news about Ms. Prissy Pants. The last I heard, she was recovering, but no one had said anything about her since then. I wanted to reach out to my contact and see what they would tell me, but I didn't. I kept thinking that no news was good news.

I also wanted to believe that the breed kept her death quiet until a suitable replacement could be made. Or perhaps, they were waiting for a deal with the president.

So far, things had quieted down on the streets. The news babbled on about the rogue humans attacking vampires, but the difference now was that they were fighting back, and human sympathizers were helping them.

I shook my head every time I saw a news report about that. Humans were so simple, so stupid. They followed the masses.

A month ago—even two weeks ago—vampires were horrible creatures that must be abolished from the earth. They should fear us, not put the breed on pedestals. They should hide from us at night, not chant 'vampires have rights too' in the streets.

They were weak and fed off the latest propaganda strewn about the airwaves and social media. It made me sick, but at the same time, I couldn't stop watching it. I sat for hours, entranced by the news reports and even the pathetic talk shows where vampires and humans were interviewed together.

I waited for the hammer to fall from the mistress and master about how the breed members should keep their mouths shut, but there was nothing so far. Another reason to believe she had fallen and Zander was finding it difficult to take over. Emotions were weak, and it didn't take a scientist to know that Zander had a lot of feelings for Kristin.

The only thing that would have been better than watching her scream in agony would have been to force her under me and fuck her while I sucked her dry. Then stake her body so she could never return.

I know it was a silly fantasy, but it was one I often had. I was a man, and her beauty was not lost on me. However, just because she had a pretty face and a killer body did not mean she could rule properly.

Adam entered the study. "I thought you might want to see the latest emails." He set down a stack of papers and eyed me warily. He expected me to lash out. It was what I had been doing all week.

"Thank you, Adam," I said with a slight smile. I needed to keep him happy. If I kept pushing him, he would eventually turn on me, and as much as I hated the weasel of a man, I needed him.

My neutral tone surprised him. "Um, you're welcome. Do you need anything else?"

"No, that will be all." He nodded and walked with a little more pep in his step. I shook my head and sighed after he left. It was such a shame that I needed him around. It was time to find someone else to be my right hand.

I retrieved the papers, standing at the desk and skimming a few. Some of the emails were from supporters, and others were from supporters who no longer stood behind me. I set those to the side. They would be dealt with swiftly.

A shiver went down my spine, and I felt like someone was watching me. I turned to look behind me, but there was nothing there. "Adam? Is that you?"

Silence greeted me, and then the feeling passed. I chalked it up to being tired. Perhaps I would go to bed early and get some extra sleep.

I was almost done reading the emails when a female voice slipped into my mind. *"It's time to sleep, Joseph."*

The hair on the back of my neck rose, and I looked around me, once again feeling like someone was watching me, but the room was empty.

I thought about the voice and realized it sounded much like the mistress. I laughed. "I must be more tired than I thought."

I set the papers aside, yawning widely and deciding I could read the rest in the morning. The letters were amusing, even the hateful ones. I made my way to my room, and once I closed the door, that odd sensation returned.

"Who is there?" I demanded, then walked around the room, peering under furniture and behind curtains, but found nothing.

"Sleep, Joseph," the female's voice spoke again, and I rubbed my eyes as they suddenly felt like I had sand in them.

I undressed and climbed into bed nude like I usually did. *"Good boy, Joseph. Now dream of me,"* the voice whispered again through my mind, and I felt myself starting to drift immediately. In the recesses of my mind, I knew something wasn't right, but I could not figure out what was off.

As I began to slip into sleep, the image of the mistress filled my mind, and I froze in my dream momentarily.

"You look surprised," she said as she walked toward the bed.

The feeling released in my body, and I sat up, letting the covers fall to my waist as I eyed her from head to toe. She was wearing a see-through black silk top and tight black pants. I recognized the outfit from pictures of her taken by the media. "I am surprised. I didn't expect you to come here. What do you want?"

She lowered her eyes, and I lifted my chin at her slight submissiveness. "I came to give myself to you."

"Why would you do that?" I asked suspiciously.

She took two more steps, approaching the bed's edge. "Because I know you were right. I was stupid to think that I could stop the war and we could live in harmony with the humans."

Her eyes were a light blue, and her dark-red hair shimmered in waves around her body. She was incredible. "It's too bad you didn't realize this sooner."

"Why do you say that?" she asked, lifting her chin slightly.

"Because you could have a man ruling beside you, not a boy."

She snickered, her eyes sparkling with mischief. "He's not a boy, Joseph. You raised him to be quite the man."

"I did," I responded, happy that she thought I did well.

"Although you might be right. Zander is rather young at heart and experience. You have been dealing with these issues for many years. You are much wiser than him."

"I'm glad you think so. It's about time you came around to my way of thinking. Too bad you're dead."

She laughed. "I'm not dead, Joseph. I am very much alive. You can see me. You can even feel me if you want."

I studied her carefully. She did look real, but then again, I knew I was dreaming.

"Do you want to touch me?"

Did I? Of fucking course, I wanted to touch her. I wanted to fuck her and live out my fantasy of draining her dry. My dick began to get hard. "Why don't you get undressed and join me in bed?" If this was a dream, I might as well take advantage of it.

She seemed happy with my suggestion and began to remove her blouse. My fingers tingled to touch her breasts and pull each of those nipples into my mouth. I would get my fill of her and then suck her dry. She dropped her blouse to the floor, then bent down to remove her high heels. Her breasts dangled forward as she did, and I almost reached out to squeeze one.

She unzipped the side zipper of her pants and began to shimmy them off her hips. I licked my lips when I saw she wore no underwear, and I could see the creamy white skin of her cunt.

My dick throbbed under the sheet, begging me to stroke it, but I remained still as she stood before me, naked and incredibly beautiful. Perhaps I wouldn't drain her yet. I would keep her around for a little while. Enjoy her body, and when I got bored with her, I would kill her then.

What great revenge that would be to take the mistress away from Zander. I almost laughed, but then she stepped forward and climbed onto the bed, crawling toward me.

"Do you dream of this often, Joseph? Do you dream of me?"

I smirked. "I have a time or two."

"I'm glad." She crawled over my legs, approaching me until our faces were only a few inches apart. "I want you, Joseph."

I peeled back the sheet covering my groin to expose my throbbing erection. "I want you, too."

She eyed my cock, then reached for it as she sat back over my legs. Her hand was cooler than I expected, but it only caused more excitement, and my head rolled back on my shoulders as I moaned.

"Oh, you did want me to touch you." She cooed toward me and stroked me more. The coolness of her hand felt good on my hot flesh, and I reached for her breasts. They, too, were cool to the touch, but they felt so fucking good in my hands.

She arched her back slightly to push her tits into my palms, and I squeezed them tighter. She whimpered as if the pain felt good, and then I wrapped my arm around her waist and pulled her body closer to suck one mound into my mouth.

One of her hands wrapped around the back of my head as she held me closer as if she were begging me for more pain. I gave it to her, biting her nipple almost to the point of breaking the skin. It was too soon to taste her blood. Soon I would do that, but not yet.

For a moment, I thought about how incredible Zander's blood always tasted. It was like an aphrodisiac, and I knew that because her blood was aged longer, it would be like opening a bottle of the finest wine.

A sound in the distance caused me to pause and pull my head back, but then Kristin took hold of my face with both hands and pulled my mouth to hers. I got lost in her kiss, feeling almost drunk as she shifted her hips forward and rubbed her pussy against my shaft.

Jesus, I needed to fuck her. The pressure in my cock was almost painful with the need to release. I squeezed her ass, pulling her harder against my dick and lifting her so I could drop her down over my cock.

I hissed as she sheathed me, and my head fell back to the headboard. Her pussy was as cold as her body, but it felt fucking incredible. It was like I was having sex with a body that had been on ice. Perhaps in this dream, she was dead, and she had come back to life for me.

I felt her body shaking, and I figured she must be close. I quickly moved and put her under me to control the entry. I held her hands over her head, yanking my hips back and slamming forward as she watched me with light-gray eyes.

She turned her face, exposing her neck, and I watched her pulse beat under the skin. My fangs instantly came down, and just as my dick threatened to erupt, I fell to her throat and slid my fangs under the skin.

The first pull of blood was the most incredible taste I had ever had, and my hips jerked forward as I felt my orgasm on the verge of happening. I greedily sucked again, filling my mouth quickly and gulping it down, but as the second mouthful began to go down, my throat began to burn.

Instinctively, I sucked more, hoping the blood I was ingesting would stop the pain, but it only worsened. I yanked my mouth away, falling to the side as I grabbed my throat and coughed.

Just as I did, the door to my bedroom burst open, and the dreamy fog around me cleared.

"What the fuck? Kristin!" I heard Zander yell, and somehow I looked to my side just in time to see her disappear.

I had no clue what was happening. I only knew I was burning from the inside out, and I screamed as I arched my body off the bed. I coughed, spewing blood over the covers around me as Zander approached.

Behind him was Angelina, and the look of glee in her eyes told me only one thing. She was happy to see me die.

"Help me!" I said around the coughing. My body felt like it was going to burn from the inside out. There had to be a way to stop this. Zander's blood could cure me.

"Help you? The only thing I will help you with is going to hell!" He raised his arms over his head, and I saw the stake in his grasp.

The pain was so intense from the blood burning through me that I did something I never expected to do as the stake began to come down. I welcomed my death.

CHAPTER TWENTY-SIX

ZANDER

I didn't think I had ever driven as fast as I did that night. We knew where he was, and we had to get to him.

Of course, my illustrious mate had to do things her own damn way too. I was not surprised that she decided to leave the compound. It made sense—scary sense.

We had to get there before she did something she couldn't handle. What did that beautiful mind of hers have her doing? She needed us there to complete the plan. We would plant the blood in a drink, and she would compel him to drink it. That was the damn plan!

Lena regularly checked in with Hugh and Corbin, and there had been no change to Kristin's condition. She also hadn't let either of them into her dream walk state. Gabe had even tried, but to no avail.

All we could do now was get there, take out Adam and anyone else on the property, and then kill Portage before she did something stupid. I frowned; what could she possibly do? She could dream walk, but that couldn't hurt the man, could it?

Hugh had sent Angelina images of the house and property, and we had no trouble locating it at the top of a hill. We parked a distance away and started through the woods on foot.

A memory flitted through my mind of a group of us going through the woods to locate Alex when Burke was holding him. Kristin was there, and at the time, she was mated to Trent, Alex's son. As we rescued Alex, Kristin had come face-to-face with her father and then drove a stake deep into his heart.

That memory seemed fitting now as we rushed toward the house as quietly as possible. I would be killing the man who had raised me. The man I had thought was my father for most of my life.

We slowed and kept our feelers out for people when we got closer. Several men were standing in the driveway, laughing about something they had seen in a movie. One walked away to patrol around the east side of the house. Another went west. Angelina and I nodded, and each went in one of those directions.

We made quick work of those two men, silently killing them before they even knew we were there. We waited for more to come to find them, and before we knew it, only Adam and Portage were left.

Both men were in the house, and Lena and I slipped inside, listening carefully for them and hoping they were unaware of our presence.

We were in luck. Adam was passed out on the couch, an empty bottle of whiskey dangling from his fingers.

Angelina raised a brow toward me, and I smiled at her and nodded for her to have the honor. I'd give her Adam as long as I could take the pleasure of staking Portage.

She smiled in glee as she tiptoed toward him. I would never know how she managed to do it so quietly in her four-inch heels. She stood over him and pulled out her stake. I thought she would slam it right into his chest, but instead, she leaned forward and hissed in his ear, "Adam, wakey, wakey, you piece of shit."

He opened bleary eyes, blinked a few times, and tensed from head to toe. The bottle in his hand fell to the ground, and I winced at the clunk it made on the marble floor.

Angelina covered his mouth with her hand as he began to open it, and then she held the stake up so he could see it. "I wanted you to see your death coming."

His eyes were wide, and she grinned, enjoying this more than she probably should. I was just about to tell her to stop playing with him when she slammed the stake into his chest, and his body erupted in ash.

She smiled at her work, then grinned my way. *"Your turn,"* she spoke into my head.

As she said that, I was already reaching out to locate Portage in the house and came up short when I felt something I had not expected.

"Do you feel Kristin?" I asked her.

She frowned, and then her eyes popped wide. *"Jesus, I do!"*

The two of us raced through the house and up a staircase. No longer were we quiet. As we approached the door, I grabbed a scent that almost took me to my knees. It was the scent of her blood, and I put my hand in my pants pocket to make sure the vial I had there had not broken. My pants were not wet, so the aroma was not coming from me.

I reached for the door and heard a gagging noise on the other side. As I threw open the door, I received the shock of my life. Straddling my nemesis was my mate.

"What the fuck? Kristin!" The words flew from my mouth as the image of her before me vanished. How the hell had she been there? Had we somehow walked into her dream state?

On the bed, Portage was coughing up blood. The scent so desirable to me because I craved it while I took my mate. How was it possible? I made a beeline to him, holding the stake over his head as he begged for my help.

With a feral growl, I slammed the stake into his chest and sucked in a deep breath as his ash blew around the room.

I stared at the ash on the bed mixed with droplets of my mate's blood.

"Did you see her?" I asked Angelina.

"Kind of hard not to see her. Although that is a sight that I did not want to see." She made a gagging noise.

"How the fuck did she do that, Lena? She was here. We aren't dreaming. How the fuck was she here?"

"I don't know, but she vanished the instant she saw us."

She came to stand next to me and reached out to wipe up a drop of blood on the sheets. She stuck her finger into her mouth. "It tastes like her."

"I could smell her before we even entered the room. I thought the vial had broken."

Angelina went still, her eyes wide as she stared into space.

"What? What's going on?"

She remained quiet for a few more seconds, snapped out of it, and grabbed my arm. "We have to get to the VMF house. Kristin is having seizures."

"What?"

She pulled me from the room. "Let's go! We have to get back to her."

The two of us raced from the room, and instead of running back through the woods to get to our transport, we took one of Portages. It wasn't like he would need them anymore.

Angelina got behind the wheel before I could even consider it, and within a second, we were racing down the winding drive and onto the main road.

"What is going on? What have they said?"

She glanced at me. "Why don't you ask Corbin? You can speak with him. I need to focus on the road."

She looked paler than usual in the dark, and I heard her swallow as if trying to get a lump out of her throat.

We would take hours to get to the VMF house and drive much of that in the daylight. I glanced to the east to see the first signs of sunrise. I peered around the vehicle, glad it was heavily tinted to protect us.

I closed my eyes, thinking back on the scene at the house. Kristin had been there. For a brief second, she had looked almost solid, but then she had faded away to nothing before my eyes.

I leaned back against the seat and reached out for Corbin. *"Corbin, what is going on?"*

"Zander." He paused. *"It's not good."*

"Tell me. Tell me the truth."

"She went into a seizure that lasted almost a minute, and then her heart stopped. I shocked her four times, and it finally started again, but she's weak, man. She is so fucking weak. I don't understand what happened."

My heart ached. *"She was there."*

"Where?"

"With Portage. When we found him, she was there with him."

"What? You saw her with him? That's impossible unless you were in her dream."

"I don't know how she did it, but she did. She was sitting in his bed, having sex with him, when we opened the door. Somehow, she materialized enough to get him to drink her blood."

"Wait a second! Was he drinking the blood that we gave you?"

"No, he had taken it straight from her vein."

"Oh, shit! That explains why her throat started bleeding as if someone had been feeding from her."

"What?"

"We were all sitting right there watching her. We knew you guys were there, and we were ready in case something happened. Suddenly, right before the seizure, she began to shake, and then two holes appeared in her throat. We had no clue what was going on. Hugh closed them, and then she went into a full-out seizure."

I fisted my hands, trying to control the avalanche of emotions about to fall. *"We are on our way back, but it will be hours before we can arrive."*

"Come as soon as you can. Isaac and Briella just got here."

"What the hell are they doing there?"

"Briella said her mother might need her."

I sighed. *"Makes sense."*

"I'm sorry, Zander. I am doing the best that I can. Hugh and I even tried to combine our energy to help repair the damage to her, but we don't have Angelina's ability."

I swallowed the lump in my throat as my eyes filled with tears. *"I appreciate all you have done."*

"I will keep going. I will keep her alive until you get here."

"Thank you," I replied, then snapped back to the car's interior.

"Corbin said she is bad." I stared out the side window.

"I'm sorry, Zander. If anyone can recover, it's Kristin."

"Yeah, I know," I said quietly, although some of me wondered if she would. Had she done more damage to her body that it would never be able to recover?

We were mostly quiet on the way to the VMF house. Occasionally, I would check in with Corbin, but the news was always the same—she was failing. We would be lucky to return before her body gave up for good.

When I contacted Corbin again to let him know we were pulling onto the property, he was closed off. I frowned, and the minute the transport was parked, I was out of the car and reaching out to find my mate.

Only I couldn't find her. I couldn't feel anything from her and I raced through the front door.

Gabe sat on the stairs, tears streaming down his face. Jett and Ryker stood off to the side, just as grief-stricken.

"No!" I yelled and rushed up the stairs to locate my mate. There was no way she could be gone!

I made it to the top floor and turned to see Corbin leaning back against the wall, his eyes closed and a somber look on his face. He turned to me, and I saw the anguish in his eyes.

I ran past him and stopped a foot into the room. Hugh lay beside her, holding her close, tears coursing down his cheeks.

"We did everything we could," he said hoarsely. "We did."

My gaze fell on the beautiful woman on the bed. Her face was as pale as snow. Her hair was as brazen as the sun. Hugh got off the bed, and I fell to my knees beside it. It couldn't be.

She couldn't be dead. I had come back for her. This was our time. She was supposed to live.

I took her hand and put it to my cheek as all the pain I had felt this last week lanced through me. A wail I had never heard left my lips, and I laid my head on the bed and sobbed.

CHAPTER TWENTY-SEVEN

KRISTIN

The sheer amount of energy it took to carry my body to this location was astounding. As I sat over my enemy, I knew this would be the last thing I would ever accomplish. My heart ached for my losses—the loved ones I would leave behind.

I begged him silently to take my blood. To end the torment of pain that I was in, and he did. He sucked from my throat like I had walked in through the front door and climbed into his bed. He drank greedily, and then it happened. The fierceness of my blood took hold and began to burn him from the inside out.

I felt vindicated and also very much alone. The moment Zander stepped into the room, I lost hold of my presence there and began to tumble. I hated that he saw that. If I could regret anything, it would be that his last living image of me would be naked on top of the man he despised.

I fell into the blackness as my body shook violently; this time, I knew there would be no coming back. I had decided to give my life for those I loved. I hoped that one day they would forgive me. I now understood why Trent had done what he had done.

I felt the sun on my face and took a moment to enjoy it before I opened my eyes. I was greeted by one of the most beautiful sunrises I had ever seen, and I stood watching as the sun grew higher into the sky. The shades of yellows, oranges, and reds were incredible to witness.

I sat cross-legged in the grass, absently pulling blades off the ground and winding them around my fingers. I heard a dog barking and knew who it was. I smiled as Garda came to my side and lay down. We sat there in peace for a long time and watched as the sun rose.

I felt a mixture of sadness and relief as I lay back in the grass, and Garda fell to his side against me. I absently brushed my hand over his coat as I thought about my life and future.

What did one do here all day?

"Whatever we want," a voice spoke from behind me, and I turned to see Alexander standing there.

"Did I say that question out loud?" I sat up, turning to him.

"No, but I always knew what you were thinking." Garda jumped up and ran to him, sitting at his side to get a pet.

I chuckled. "I guess you did."

He came to my side and sank onto the grass, putting his arms over his knees. "So you decided, huh?"

"I guess I did."

"You sure? You are giving up a lot, Kris."

"I know, but I think I overdid it. I might have pushed my body a little too hard."

He laughed. "You were always one to do that."

"Yeah." I chuckled.

"At least you accomplished your goal."

"I did," I said proudly.

He stared at my profile. "I hate to say this, but I don't think you should be here."

"What do you mean?"

"I mean, most of us, when we die, are reborn almost immediately. Well, unless we are staked, and then it becomes a little more final."

"Okay," I said slowly. "What does that mean? Do you think someone staked me?"

He shook his head. "No, I know they didn't." He turned to face me and took my hand. "I think you are being given another chance."

"A chance to do what?"

"To return to your life."

I frowned. "But I died. I know I did."

"Yes, you are dead, but you shouldn't be here, Kris. Despite me wanting you to be here, the door is still open for you to return."

I glanced around, chuckling. "I don't see any doors."

Alex pulled my hand closer to him. "Kristin, you have been given a chance to have the man you love, to rule over our breed in a time of great change. You have the opportunity to make a difference. Do you want to pass that up?"

"I'm tired, Alex. I am tired of always having to make decisions that affect everyone. Tired of being this person who everyone looked up to. I'm exhausted." I stared at him. "You never told me how exhausting it would be."

He sighed. "I know how exhausting it can be, Kris. I also know that you have the power and energy to do it. Besides, you wouldn't be doing it alone anymore. You have Zander at your side and Angelina, Hugh, and Corbin to help you. You could delegate to them and let them be part of it."

"I'm not very good at letting others take over."

He tweaked my nose. "You are a control freak, but that is what we all love about you. You take it all on, and you never let anyone down."

"I do. I let many people down."

"Not really. I think you let yourself down more than others. You expect more from yourself. You need to lighten up a bit."

I turned and looked out over the rolling hills in front of me. "Maybe."

"There is no maybe about it, Kris." He released my hand, stood, reached down, and pulled me to my feet. "They need you. Can you not hear the cries from below? Can you not feel the agony of your loss? Listen carefully."

I closed my eyes, and I could feel the pain deep inside me. I could hear the sobbing, which tore at my heart and brought tears to my eyes.

"They need you, Kris." He took hold of my face. "You can stay here if that is what you want, or you can return to them now. Let me ask you a question, and if the answer is no, then you stay."

"Okay, what is the question?"

"Do you love them? Do you love every one of them and want to be part of their lives? Do you want to watch your children grow? Do you want to see them happy and help with their struggles? Do you want to give up your chance to have the man you have always loved? Do you want to give that up?"

"That was more than one question," I joked but then grew serious. I thought about what Alex asked, and my will to live grew stronger with each answer to one of those questions. I shook my head. "No, I don't want to live without them. I don't want to lose what I had."

He leaned forward and kissed me tenderly once, his emerald-green eyes shining with moisture. "Then go home, Kristin. Go home and be with them." He stepped back and put his hands on my shoulders. "Go home."

With that, he pushed me gently back, and I began to fall again. The brightness around me was replaced by darkness, and when I landed, I gasped for breath, and my eyes flashed open.

I stared at the ceiling and then shifted my head to the left. Every muscle in my body ached, but pure joy radiated out of me as my eyes landed on the man I adored. Zander sat on his knees, his beautiful blue eyes wide as he stared at me. Another person stood behind him, my sister, looking just as shocked as Zander.

"Kristin?" Zander croaked, and my gaze went back to his.

"Zander," I whispered.

"Oh my god! Kristin!" He burst to his feet and flung himself on the bed, wrapping his arms around me as he laughed and cried. He took my face in his hands. "Don't you fucking leave me again! Do you hear that? Don't you do that again!"

Angelina was on my other side, and I heard feet pounding down the hallway. The room quickly filled, and each one looked more astonished than the last.

"I don't understand how you came back, but I am so glad you did," Angelina said as she squeezed my arms. Corbin and Hugh shook their heads as they approached the bed to stand behind her.

"How is this possible?" Hugh asked.

I smiled at him. "Someone important reminded me what I had to lose if I didn't come back."

"What would you lose?" Corbin asked.

I glanced at the door to see Isaac step in, Briella in his arms. I squeezed Zander's hand. "All of you, my family."

EPILOGUE

KRISTIN

Two months had passed since I returned from the dead, and not a day went by that I wasn't thankful for Alex's encouragement to return.

I discovered I had been without a heartbeat for over an hour, which was quite a marvel. I didn't understand how it happened, and neither did anyone else, but we were all thankful for the miracle of my return.

The day after I woke, I felt strong enough to rekindle my mating bond with Zander. The moment I did, my body began to rebuild more vigorously than ever. Two days later, I was out of bed and back to figuring things out.

Portage was gone for good, and none of us understood how I had been able to feed him straight from my vein, but if there was anything I had learned in my life, it was that impossible things could be possible if you wanted them bad enough. Zander had made me promise I would never do that again and teased me about having sex with my enemy. I ensured he knew that I had hated every moment and that he was the only one I wanted in my bed for the rest of our long lives.

Four days later, I conceived a child with Zander, and Briella quickly told me that her brother, Kellan, would be as strong and incredible as she was.

Her other brothers, Rex and Garrett, had been happy to see I survived. We didn't tell them what really happened. That information stayed within the group that had witnessed my miracle.

When Portage died, Garrett had confessed to having been compelled by him. He had a lot of guilt for passing along sensitive information to our enemy, but Garrett was still young and had yet to complete his transition. He was easy to compel, and we decided that while we typically waited for our males to be in their thirties when they turned, we would turn Garrett soon.

Briella said that my and Angelina's children would be critical to the future. My sister would have two more, one born from each mate. Angelina didn't know this yet, but Briella was happy to share the juicy gossip with me.

I stood before the mirror, putting my hair up and ensuring my makeup was perfect. Tonight was a big night, and I couldn't wait to celebrate.

Zander appeared behind me, his mouth immediately going to my neck, one hand covering my still flat belly. "God, you look good enough to eat."

"You're going to have to wait, Master."

He chuckled. "That's mean, Mistress."

I turned in his arms and kissed him passionately. "It's mean to both of us, but the president should be here soon. I need to make sure everything is ready."

"It's ready. The house looks beautiful, just like you."

I hiked a brow. "You are comparing me to a house?"

He chuckled. "No. That's not what I meant."

"You better not have," I scolded him playfully.

The two of us went down the stairs shortly after, and I looked over the decorations as we went. We had crews working night and day the last two weeks to ensure the house was perfect. If I didn't know any better, I would say the damage had never been done here at the VMF house.

A few minutes later, Ryker told me the president had arrived. This was not the first time we had met since I woke up. Over the last few weeks, I traveled to Washington several times.

I went to the front door and welcomed him, his wife, and their two children with open arms. He also brought along some other important people. They no longer feared me, and we had grown a wonderful friendship based on trust and the need to protect those who followed us. I knew our future was safe for a while—or at least until the next president took over.

During the evening, we mingled—vampires and humans. It reminded me of the old days, and my eyes slipped to Mick, who once had been one of my human visitors. Then my gaze shifted to Olivia and Gabe, and I smiled. So many years with those people, so many stories. From human tragedies to vampire tales.

There was so much love in this room. So many friendships and stories to share. I stood before the fireplace and let my eyes drift over the picture I had hung back up there. My eyes landed on Alex, and I smiled. I will forever be grateful to him, not only because he convinced me to return but because he believed in me.

Zander put his hand on my lower back as he paused by me. "We should take another one of those."

"What? Tonight?"

He shrugged. "Yeah, why not? That picture was a turning point. New friends and old friends coming together."

I grinned at him, leaned forward, and kissed him. "I love it."

"And I love you," he responded in a husky voice.

We gathered everyone together, and this time, we were packed on the staircase. There was double the number of people in this one, but that was good.

The president and his family stood beside me in the middle of the staircase. To my left was Zander. Right behind me was Hugh holding Briella, with Garrett and Rex beside him. Angelina and Corbin were right in front of us, and in front of them were Gideon and Paxton who had quickly mated once we returned.

Angelina was taking over the head of the Vampire Military Force so someone was ready to respond when one of our breed, or a group of humans, got out of control. Corbin, Hugh, and Gideon would be helping her. Zander and I were going to be busy dealing with the logistics of the White House and Congress, along with Clayton and Cameron.

The rest of our friends, families, sentinels, and guests of the president filled in around us. One of the secret service men took the pictures.

I looked forward to seeing the images blown up and promised the president I would give him a copy.

After that, glasses were raised in a toast, and the president spoke. "To new beginnings, new friendships, and to changes in the world that will only be for the better."

Through it all, my daughter Briella observed from the safety of either Hugh's arms or Isaac's. Later in the evening, she finally came to me, looking sleepy. She might be brilliant, but her body was still that of a baby.

She leaned her head against mine. *"I never got a chance to ask how you managed to come back."*

I chuckled into her head. *"You might be intelligent, Briella. You can see the future and make decisions based on facts, but there is one thing you do not understand yet."*

"What could I not understand?"

I stared into my daughter's eyes. *"You can't possibly understand what love can do and how strong of a force it can be."*

"Perhaps not." She yawned, and I tucked her close to my chest, feeling happier than I ever had.

"Stick with me, little one, and I will teach you."

As I took her up the steps to her room, I glanced back, and a wave of emotion crashed over me. I had felt I was missing something all my life, but not anymore. Now I had it all and knew my blood would be blue forever.

THE END

A NOTE TO READERS:

In 2010, I decided to write a book. That was the first book I had ever written, and I had never entertained the idea of creating such a thing. With the birth of that book, so began my passion for writing.

The first book was *My Blood Runs Blue*, and in that story, I created a world of vampires unlike any other world created. How the vampires were created, how they reacted to humans, and even how they smelled to each other came from my fantasies.

Shortly after the first book, I wrote *Blue Blood For Life*. There were a few years between that book and the next, and that third book became the second in the series to explain how Kristin got to where she was. During that time, I rewrote parts of the series' first two books and then quickly went on to write *Mixing the Blue Blood* and *Blue Bloods Final Destiny*.

As I was writing that final book, I realized I wasn't ready to let Kristin go. She was a police officer who gave everything to protect those she swore an oath to. Kristin was me, and I wasn't ready to let go of who she was and what she had become. So I did the only thing a writer can do; I created another world and spun Kristin off into Blue Blood Returns 40 years later.

With this new series, I could bring new life to the stories. I could intertwine pieces of the past and introduce new characters. Kristin is still the lead, but her sister is right beside her. New and old faces were together where questions from the original series, never answered, finally were.

The new series was darker, grittier, and much steamier than the first one, but that is what I saw for my characters in the future.

In this final book, *The Reckoning*, I had a hard time. I knew what needed to happen but struggled to get the characters to behave. I started and stopped this book several times over months. I realized that one of the things that held me back was knowing that I would have to say goodbye to these characters.

Kristin was no longer a cop in this book, and neither am I. It took me a while, but I finally realized that both Kristin and I needed to move on. It was time to let the past become the past and move on to new things.

I have already been asked by some earlier readers if there will ever be another spin-off, and the answer to that question is, I honestly do not know. Did I leave it where I could jump into the future? Yes. But will I? Who knows. Only time will tell. For now, I will step away from the paranormal world and finish a few other books that need my attention.

For all of you who have followed the stories of Blue Blood through the years, I thank you. You will never know how much it has meant to me to share these stories with you.

Now, it's time to say goodbye to Kristin, Zander, Alex, Gabe, Olivia, Angelina, Trent, Hugh, and Garda and turn the page.

At least for now—

ABOUT THE AUTHOR

Stacy Eaton began her writing career in October of 2010 and, as each year goes by, she releases more and more novels. Stacy took an early retirement from law enforcement after over fifteen years of service, with her last three in investigations and crime scene investigation.

Stacy resides in southeastern Pennsylvania with her husband, who works in law enforcement. She has a daughter in college, and a son who is currently serving in the United States Navy. She also has two grandchildren.

Stacy volunteers with several organizations to help with awareness of PTSD, suicide, addiction and homelessness for veterans. She is also a National Trainer for a company that teaches Active Shooter Response Options for businesses, schools, healthcare and religious organization.

Stacy is also involved in Domestic Violence Awareness and served on the Board of Directors for her local Domestic Violence Center for three years.

Be sure to visit www.stacyeaton.com for updates and more information on her books.

Sign up for all the latest information on Stacy's Newsletter!

STACY BOOKS - PAPERBACK

Rise Again Warrior Series

The *Rise Again Warrior Series* is an intense and emotional journey through the lives of many service members, their families, and their friends. Focusing on the trials that they face after wartime is over, and they have returned home to a nation that sometimes seems to have forgotten what they were fighting for, and what all of these people sacrificed in the name of Honor & Duty. Books Include: Mission: Believe, Mission:Accept, Mission: Repair, Mission: Courage and Mission: Gratitude

Loving a Young Series

The *Loving a Young Series* is a steamy romance series that consists of six books. While these books are all standalone romances, the characters will be seen across the series since this is a small-town romance series about siblings finding forever loves.

Books include: Wesley, Henley, Riley, Kayley & Bradley

The Loving a Winston Series

The *Loving a Winston Series* is a five-book steamy romance series that spins off of the *Loving a Young Series*. Characters from both series will appear from book to book. Each book is a standalone romance with suspense and spicy romance scenes.

Books Include: Cara, Evan, Candy, Coral and Carmen.

The Unexpected Series

The *Unexpected Series* is a steamy romance series where anything can happen and probably will. Each book in the series is a stand-alone happily ever after, or happy for now book. While they are stand-alone, the books are all centered around Safety Zone Security and the employees there. Characters from one book will continue throughout the rest of the series. Books Include: Unexpected Packages, Unexpected Arrivals, Unexpected Trouble, Unexpected Storms, Unexpected Desires, Unexpected Ties.

Paranormal Romance:

My Blood Runs Blue Series

My Blood Runs Blue Series is an adult Paranormal Action/Romance Series with vampires and is intended for mature audiences.

Books Include: My Blood Runs Blue, The Pulse of Blue Blood, Blue Blood for Life, Mixing the Blue Blood, Blue Bloods Final Destiny,

The Return of Blue Blood Series:

This series is 40 years in the future after My Blood Runs Blue. It is a very steamy series intended for mature audiences.

Books Included: Kristin: Blue Blood Returns, Hugh: Blue Blood Compelled, Zander: Blue Blood Reborn, Lena: Blue Blood Desired, Reckoning, Blue Blood Finale

The Twisted Love Series

with Amy Manemann Co-Author

The Twisted Love Series is a continuing Saga of intense police procedures and romantic suspense and contains nine books in total. It delves deep into the world of crime and how it is investigated. Due to that fact, the crimes continue from one book to the next and could leave you hanging till the next one. Not all crimes are solved in the pages of one book. These books also contain strong adult language, violence, and sexual situations. Books Included: Love Lorn, Love Torn, Love Inked, Love Drowned, Love Carved, Love Trapped, Love Crossed, Love Twisted, Love Lies.

Single Titles

Whether I'll Live or Die

You're Not Alone

Garda ~ Welcome to the Realm

Liveon ~ No Evil

Second Shield

Distorted Loyalty

Six Days of Memories

Second Shield II: The Return

Tempt Me Too

Finding the Strength

Finding Love in Special Places:

Stacy's Short Story Series

Sweet Romance about adult topics. Stories include: Finding Love on Christmas Vacation, Finding Love on the Summer Surf, Finding Love with Dear Santa, Finding Love with a Champagne Toast, Finding Love on the High Seas

Heart of the Family Series

The *Heart of the Family* Series is a small-town steamy romance series that is best read in order. Books Include:

Mistletoe & Cocoa Kisses, Roses & Champagne Kisses, Orchids & Hurricane Kisses, Carnations & Hot Toddy Kisses,

Heal Me Series

Love Spicy Medical Romance? Check out the rest of the Heal Me Series for sexy romances that will warm your heart as they deal with life-altering medical and psychological issues. These books do contain language and open door sexual relations. While each book in the Heal Me Series is a stand-alone book, the characters cross between books and are best enjoyed by reading them in order. Books Include: Cured, Revived, Mended and Rescued.

The Celebration Series

The Celebration Series: Celebration Township is made for family, friends, falling in love, and don't forget celebrating the holidays. The first twelve books bring two people onto center stage as they overcome odds and figure out what their futures may hold. There is laughter, love, romance and even suspense when you join these couples as they each find a happily ever after over a holiday. The thirteenth book brings all twelve couples, and even a few special guests, into final focus as the first couple in Tangled in Tinsel prepares for their wedding one year after they met. Books Include: Tangled in Tinsel, Tears to Cheers, Heathens to Hearts, Rainbows Bring Riches, Sweet as Sugar, Making Mom Mad, Sparklers or Spankings, Raffles to Rattles, Flirting with Fireworks, Working Under Wheels, Masquerading at Midnight, Blessing & Beans, Velvet & Vows.

The Sometimes Series:

The Sometimes Series consists of three romances where the passion is a touch spicy and there is a hint of suspense is in the air. Sometimes You Win is a stand-alone story that ends with a Happy-for-Now ending. Sometimes you Lose, Book 2 of the series does end in a cliffhanger and Sometimes You Play the Game will finally give the couple a Happily Ever After. In all three books, you will find adult language and situations. Books Include: Sometimes You Win, Sometimes you Lose, Sometimes You Play The Game.

Pleasure Your Fantasies Series

The Pleasure Your Fantasies series is an ADULT Series with coarse language and intense sexual situations along with suspense. Books Include: Mistletoe Fantasies, Whispered Fantasies, Secret Fantasies, and more coming in 2022.

List Updated 1/18/22